"I don't wa... rich girl to give up on me and leave."

The words made Tracey's eyes sting and she couldn't look at Ty.

This was too wonderful, too special. She couldn't believe they were talking to each other like this, that Ty was hinting that her approval of him might be as important to him as his approval was to her.

If this was a dream, she didn't want to wake up. She didn't let herself think of the things about her that he could never approve of, because she needed this moment too much; her soul was starved for it....

What kind of man makes the perfect husband?

A man with a big heart and strong arms—someone tough
but tender, powerful yet passionate....

And where can such a man be found?

Marriages made on the ranch...

Susan Fox lives with her youngest son, Patrick, in
Des Moines, Iowa, U.S.A. A lifelong fan of Westerns and
cowboys, she tends to think of romantic heroes in terms of
Stetsons and boots! In what spare time she has, Susan is an
unabashed couch potato and movie fan. She particularly
enjoys romantic movies, and also reads a variety of romance
novels—with guaranteed happy endings—and plans to
write many more of her own.

THE MAN SHE'LL MARRY

Susan Fox

TORONTO • NEW YORK • LONDON
AMSTERDAM • PARIS • SYDNEY • HAMBURG
STOCKHOLM • ATHENS • TOKYO • MILAN • MADRID
PRAGUE • WARSAW • BUDAPEST • AUCKLAND

ISBN 0-373-03648-5

THE MAN SHE'LL MARRY

First North American Publication 2001.

CHAPTER ONE

THE San Antonio nightspot was crowded and loud. The dance floor was a veritable sea of bodies. Colored lights flickered and flashed and bounced rapidly over the dancers.

Tracy LeDeux watched it all through jaded eyes. Somehow everyone seemed to be trying too hard to have a good time. Their movements were too enthusiastic, their laughter too loud, their high spirits too forced.

Just like hers.

She glanced across the table at her date and saw the predatory gleam in his eyes. Gregory Parker III was movie star handsome. Unfortunately, he knew it. His fine Southern manners had turned out to be a thin veneer. No wasn't a word he'd heard often in his life of privilege and he was unhappy about her refusal to go home with him. He'd spent a small fortune on her that evening and it was clear that he expected a return on his investment.

Whether she felt like giving it to him or not. Why hadn't she seen what he was like before she'd agreed to go out with him?

Because she hadn't wanted to see it. She knew almost no one in San Antonio, and she'd been bored and lonely. One more solitary night in her penthouse might have sent her over the edge. Gregory III had provided a welcome distraction. But five minutes after they'd sat down to a fine dinner she'd realized she might have done better to go over the edge.

She had to resist the urge to lean away when Greg surged close to her, his whiskey breath strong in her face.

"It's late, Tracy. Let's go to my place, have a drink." Greg smiled at her the way vain, handsome men smiled when they were determined to get something. This was a man who'd got by on his looks and his family's money, a man too spoiled to be truly interested in pleasing anyone but himself. Which was why he'd ignored both of her earlier refusals to the same suggestion.

Tracy made herself smile at him, a playful, chiding smile she hoped would appease him. "It's not that late, Greg. I need to go to the ladies' room."

Just that quickly, she escaped him. She managed it so swiftly that she'd caught only the start of another of his spoiled little boy frowns. There was a telephone in the ladies' lounge. She would call a cab and go home. Later she could claim sudden illness. It was the coward's way out, but she'd seen the hint of anger in Greg's gaze, and he'd been drinking heavily. Some scrap of self-preservation warned her that the moment they were away from other people he would drop any pretense of gentlemanly behavior.

The tall cowboy who collided with her in the crowd was dressed no differently than half the men in the nightclub. But he was tall—huge—his six foot plus height making her feel as small as a child. Her impact against his hard body sent a flash of heat through her and she glanced up in surprise. But the moment she saw who it was beneath that white dress Stetson, her heart shriveled.

Ty Cameron was one of the most ruggedly handsome millionaire oilman/ranchers in Texas. His blond hair was a bright mix of bronze and wheat and white from the sun, and when combined with his sun-darkened skin and the deep vivid blue of his eyes, he was striking.

Tracy had never felt so petite and feminine as in that unexpected moment of impact. But the instant she saw the cold light of recognition in his gaze, she felt sick. The world took a sudden dip. If he hadn't taken hold of her arms to steady her, the shock of seeing him—of *him* seeing *her*— might have made her faint. She was so profoundly ashamed of what he knew about her—of what he must think—that she wanted to disappear.

Her ever-present guilt spiked high on a fresh tide of regret. She'd hoped to never see him again. She should have known she'd have to leave Texas to ensure that.

Her shaky, ''Pardon me,'' acknowledged nothing more than their accidental collision. She pulled away from him, relieved beyond words when his hands fell away and the low-voltage current of his touch was no longer sending tiny shocks over her skin.

She would have run from him if she could, but the crowd was too dense for her to accomplish more than a slow retreat as she wove between bodies to put as much space between her and Ty Cameron as possible. At last she reached the ladies' lounge and made her call. But the news that she might be in for a forty-five minute wait upset her even more.

What were her chances of leaving the nightclub and finding a cab on her own? She'd hardly ever waited for a cab. But then, she'd rarely called for one after midnight. She dreaded the thought of standing on the street at this time of night waiting to flag down a taxi.

If she was gone too long, Greg might come looking for her. The last thing she wanted was for him to find her standing alone outside. She'd have to go back to the table, wait a few minutes, then excuse herself to go back to the ladies' room. Then she could slip out. A second trip might lend credence to her later plea of illness.

The new complication was Ty Cameron. If she went back to the table, she might see him again.

The idea made her nerves crackle with anxiety. Hopefully the place was too crowded for a second encounter. Perhaps now that he knew she was around, he would avoid her. She was certain he wanted to see her even less than she wanted to see him.

Resigned to the perils in her plan to escape, Tracy checked her hair and makeup. The sight of her pale face in the mirror gave her another shock. Her eyes were puffy, her complexion unnaturally flushed and blotchy. She'd been drinking too much lately, and it was beginning to show.

It had started with a nerve-calming glass of wine on nights when insomnia plagued her. Now she couldn't sleep without it. She was terrified she was becoming an alcoholic, but she didn't seem to have the strength to do anything about it. She wasn't certain anymore that she was worth the effort. The sick feeling of doom panicked her and drove her to exit the lounge to lose herself in the noise of the nightclub.

It was almost a relief to reach her table. She'd not caught so much as a glimpse of Ty Cameron. Perhaps he'd been on his way out of the nightspot. She'd been too rattled to notice if he'd been with anyone.

Ty Cameron watched the petite blonde. Tracy looked thinner than when he'd last seen her. She was all huge blue eyes and blond hair. And legs. Perfect legs. She still looked as vulnerable as a child, still carried that lost look. He'd heard she'd parted ways with her poison-pill mother, so maybe Tracy had wised up. Maybe the huge inheritance she'd come into had given her a choice.

Though she'd made up for the terrible things she'd done, the fact that she'd done them in the first place indicated a character flaw he couldn't abide. He figured she was as wicked and worthless as her mother. Or soon would be.

Nevertheless, as he watched her return to her table and saw that she was with Parker, he felt a glimmer of sympathy. He could read her blue eyes as if they were flashing neon letters a foot tall, and what he read in them was worry.

She ought to worry. Parker fancied himself a ladies' man and he preferred fragile blondes. Tracy LeDeux was in for a night of sex-capades, though if she was as much like her soulless mother as he thought, she was promiscuous enough to handle it.

He was about to look away from Tracy and dismiss her presence altogether when he noticed her drink slip from her fingers. The glass tumbled to the table, but Tracy stared at it numbly. Her lashes fell shut heavily, then opened.

She turned her head to glance at her date, but she swayed with the movement. Parker reached over suddenly to steady her. Ty couldn't have missed the gleam of anticipation in Parker's smile. Or the woozy distress on Tracy's face.

The dizziness had come over her suddenly. She was so weak, so horribly uncoordinated. The narrow tunnel that had shrunk the room grew darker and narrower with every hard beat of her heart. The terror she felt was overwhelming as the world swam away in a gray haze.

Tracy's first coherent thought was that she felt safe. Cocooned. In spite of a faint headache, she felt an odd peace.

It was that strange sense of safety and peace that made her rouse herself. She rarely felt safe, and peace was a foreign sensation. The heavy guilt that had weighted her heart for so long had banished any sense of ease or genuine self-worth.

Was she truly awake or was she dreaming? She rolled to her back in the big bed and forced her eyes open, struggling to cling to the warm feelings. But the moment she got her eyes to focus, that rare sense of safety and peace vanished. *This was not her bedroom.*

The events of the night before came roaring back. Greg Parker's face swam in her memory like a ghoul. The last thing she remembered was him advancing on her, picking her up, then…nothing. *Nothing!*

The mad whirl of terror made her stomach churn. She started to fling off the sheet and comforter to race for the bathroom, then froze as a second traumatic revelation pounded into her brain: *she wasn't wearing her dress!*

The horror she felt burst out of her in a panicked sound of distress and she clutched the bedclothes to herself.

The rough male voice that sounded from the foot of the bed made her jump.

"Here."

She barely had time to glance in the direction of the voice before a thick white terry-cloth robe came sailing through the air at her.

"Put that on and get cleaned up. Your dress is on a hook in the bathroom."

Ty Cameron stood at the foot of the bed like an Old West lawman who'd tracked down an outlaw he meant to lynch. Contempt glinted in his cold gaze. The shock of his presence was quickly swallowed up by overwhelming mortification.

Shame made her voice a raspy little croak. "Wh-where am I?"

Ty's harsh mouth quirked. "Sober up and figure it out."

The words were a slap that sent scorching heat into her face. She felt the hurt to her soul when the look in his eyes suddenly switched to indifference. It was a look that let her know she'd been judged and found so in want that she wasn't worth another second of his attention.

As if to underscore the impression, he turned from her and walked to the door. He closed it behind him with a finality that shook her.

The chill that descended sliced into her heart like a shard of ice. She was contemptible, unredeemable. With one look and a few terse words, Ty Cameron had somehow confirmed her secret fears about herself and her dark terrors about how her life would go.

She was wealthy, close to obscenely wealthy. At almost twenty-three, she was young and she still had her looks, but her life was worth nothing. She had no one. She had no real stability, no ambition, and no place to belong. There was no point to her life, no compelling reason to exist.

If she died at that moment, she wasn't certain anyone but her mother would care. Even then, the only thing Ramona would want to know when she found out her only child was dead was whether Tracy had made a will and left her money.

Somehow, Tracy managed to mute her despairing thoughts. She had to pull herself together. Solving the mystery of what had happened to her and how she'd ended up with Ty Cameron was a distant second to the frantic need to get away from him.

*   *   *

Once she'd showered, brushed her teeth with the
new toothbrush laid out, and tried to do something
with her hair, Tracy hurried silently through the
huge, single-story ranch house. She reached the
large red-tiled entry hall and came to a shaky halt.

She knew she was at Cameron Ranch, but that
also meant she was miles from San Antonio. She
had no car and no way to leave.

Unless she could call a car rental agency and
have a car delivered. Her heart sank. She'd need a
credit card number for that, and all she had in her
small evening bag was her driver's license, a few
cosmetics, and the key to her penthouse.

The deep voice that carried from the direction
of the dining room sent her panic higher.

"Come in and get something to eat."

The invitation was nothing more than basic good
manners. Ty Cameron was the kind of man who'd
at least feed a ratty stray before he chased it off or
sent it to the pound. A touch of compassion, but
an unwavering determination to do nothing more
than was humane. And for all her money, Tracy
LeDeux was the ratty stray.

Tracy started toward the sound of his voice on
reluctant feet. Oh God, she'd hate to see his harsh
face, to see the condemnation in his eyes. He despised her. Then again, she despised herself, so at
least they agreed on something.

More of the events of the night before had come

back to her, though she still didn't recall anything after she'd felt the dizziness and Greg had zoomed close and picked her up.

What was clear was that whatever had happened next, Ty Cameron had brought her to his ranch and put her to bed. Somehow he'd cut Gregory III out of the equation.

She hoped it had been before Greg had succeeded at anything. Logic told her that although her head pounded, she felt queasy, and her nerves were on edge, there were no other physical aftereffects of the night before. No permanent consequences, no sexual shame to endure. At least not from last night.

But her terror of being that vulnerable undermined logical thought. Since it was clear to her now that Greg had drugged her, how much more had he done to rob her of choice? Black memories stirred and she felt their poison rise.

A wave of dizzy fear made her falter at the wide doorway into the large, formal dining room.

If Greg had violated her, he must have discarded her in some public place, which accounted for Ty's rescue. And Ty was a man of the world. He'd know at a glance what had been done to her. Oh God...

"You should see a doctor."

Ty's grim words were somehow a veiled confirmation of her worst fears. Tracy put out a hand to the door frame, her knees trembling almost too much to hold her up.

"D-did he..." She couldn't put her worst fear into words. She struggled to make herself look at Ty's stern face and braced herself for his answer.

Ty sat at the head of the polished table that was set for lunch. He wore the usual cowboy clothes, denim and chambray, and by now he'd probably put in a half day's work. His hard gaze took her in, then settled on her pale face and sharpened. He knew what she was asking.

"Did he what? Take what you offered?"

Emotion stung her eyes but she held it back. "I didn't."

Cynicism flashed over his handsome face. "What did you think would happen when you got drunk with someone like Parker? No one's that naïve."

Tracy's heart quivered with hurt. She swallowed convulsively and fought for a scrap of dignity.

"I need to get back to San Antonio. C-can I use your phone?" She hated that she'd stuttered. Hated that she'd shown him anything of the shamed horror in her soul.

"You can borrow a car. I'll have it picked up later." He nodded toward the place that had been set for her at the table. "Come in and have something to eat."

Tracy knew absolutely that she wouldn't be able

to swallow a bite of food. Not Ty Cameron's food, not at his table, and certainly not under his condemning gaze. At the mercy of whatever devastating remark he'd make next.

"I need to go home now. I have to be somewhere."

The lie made everything so much worse. It was another grim weight on a conscience already too heavily burdened.

And Ty could tell it was a lie. The way he looked at her said so. The fact that he didn't challenge it or remark on it let her know that honesty wasn't a reasonable expectation where she was concerned.

Ty leaned back in his chair and slid a hand into his jeans pocket. He held up the keys he pulled out.

"The silver Cadillac at this end of the garage," he said, then tossed her the keys. Tracy caught them, amazed she'd been able to do it.

Ty's eyes sharpened on her again. "Good. You've got decent reflexes and coordination. People on the roads will be safe."

That's when she understood that tossing her the keys had been a test rather than a careless demonstration of disrespect.

"Park it in a good spot where it won't get hit," he went on. "Put the keys under the seat, lock them in, then call and leave a message where to pick it up.''

Which meant that he didn't want to see her again, didn't care to speak to her personally, hence the precise instructions. Because he meant to drive home the notion that he couldn't stand her, that she was dirt under his boots.

Her soft, ''Thank you,'' was brittle. His vivid gaze held hers ruthlessly and she couldn't seem to look away. He was searching deep, and probably seeing too much. It was a cinch he didn't detect anything of value.

Tracy turned and walked away with as much outward dignity as she could summon. It was faked, of course. Just like almost everything she showed the world.

She let herself out the front door of the big ranch house, then winced. The noon sun was brutally bright. And hot. Hot enough to make her stomach pitch and the world go blurry. Her knees felt rubbery by the time she walked to the big garage and let herself in the side door. The dimness inside relieved only a little of the pain in her head.

Once inside the Cadillac, she adjusted the seat then couldn't get the key in the ignition. Frustration made her fumbling worse. She was a wreck. Was she in any condition to drive back to town?

The alternative—that she'd have to face Ty

again and seek his help—made her struggle to steady her hand and match the key to the ignition. This time, she succeeded. The big engine purred to life and she gave a relieved sigh. She could do this.

Tracy found the garage door remote on the visor and pressed the button. The big door motored open and she pushed the visor up.

But the visor dropped back down. The remote clipped to it fell into her lap. Tracy dutifully picked it up and clipped it on the visor before she turned to look over her shoulder to back the big car out of the garage. The sudden movement made her dizzy, but she ignored the feeling. The car rolled only a yard or so before the visor again tipped down and the remote again fell into her lap.

She should have left the remote where it fell or tossed it to the dash. Instead, she clipped it to the visor, pushed the visor up, then turned dizzily to continue slowly backing the car.

It moved only a couple of feet before she sensed the visor begin to tip down. Still turned to watch where she was going, she threw up her hand to keep it in place. Impatience made her hit the visor with more force than she'd intended.

And she must have triggered the button on the remote because the big door started down, though Tracy didn't realize that until she saw the bottom edge of the door lower into sight.

Everything went weirdly wrong then. Still turned to back out, Tracy pressed down on the brake. At the same time, she felt for the remote on the visor and pressed the button, thinking the door would reverse and go up.

But the door didn't stop. Alarmed, Tracy shoved down on the brake, but her foot slipped off the edge and the heel strap of her shoe caught. She jerked her shoe free and jabbed desperately for the brake.

She was too dizzy and uncoordinated to locate the brake pedal, but panic helped her manage it. Or so she thought. She'd expected to stop the car, so it was a shock when the big vehicle lurched backward. The massive door scraped heavily onto the trunk as it pressed relentlessly downward. The squawk of metal heightened her hysteria as the door scraped deeper along the trunk then hit the back glass of the car.

Car and door strained against each other, defying her effort to stop the nightmare as she made a last jab for the brake pedal. Suddenly the big car engine roared and the garage door popped out of its tracks.

In that next split second, Tracy realized she'd been pressing the accelerator. Horrified, she turned to face the windshield, pulled her foot off the gas and made a new try for the brake. The loud crash of the big door collapsing on the car roof was as loud as an explosion.

And then came the silence, that awful silence as the car idled peacefully and Tracy fought to understand what had happened. The wild staccato that pounded her ears was the sound of a heart gone crazy with terror.

Park it where it won't get hit.

Ty's grim instruction came back to her like a klaxon alarm of imminent doom.

CHAPTER TWO

THE hard rocking of the big car penetrated her shock. Dazed, Tracy turned her head to see a blur of blue outside the window.

Ty was yanking powerfully on the handle to open the jammed car door. Another half-dozen pulls and it gave. The door squealed open. Ty surged toward her and Tracy shrank back. Alarmed, she reflexively threw up her arm to protect herself. The back of her hand hit Ty's jaw, but the brutal strike she'd hysterically imagined coming her way didn't happen.

It took a second to register that Ty had been grabbing for the ignition to switch off the idling car. In the sudden silence of the engine, Tracy's horrified gaze met his furious one in the close confines.

She saw the instant he understood her protective move and took offense. Now the furious blue of his eyes went livid and a dark flush deepened his tan. His voice was gritty with control.

"I've never struck a woman in my life, Tracy, however tempting it might be."

Tracy shivered at his low tone. And then she noticed the nick on his jaw and watched in fresh horror as blood welled into the small wound. Her ring had done that, she realized, sickened. Oh God!

The quick snap of the seat belt release was her only warning before she found herself hauled out of the car and deposited on her feet out of the way. Her legs felt too weak when Ty released her. She swayed, in danger of falling to the concrete floor before she braced her hand against the wall behind her.

Tracy watched Ty's grim inspection of the disaster and prayed to die, but God ignored this fervent petition just as steadfastly as He'd ignored those other times she'd prayed it. She cringed at the low, rumbling sound of Ty's voice as he muttered a series of swear words.

Tracy couldn't fault him for his fury. His beautiful silver Cadillac was ruined. The big door had scraped heavily the length of the trunk and smashed the back glass before the door had slipped the track and collapsed full-length on the car, pushing down the roof. The hood was dented almost as ruinously as the trunk. The windshield hadn't shattered, but the glass was a mass of cracks.

"I'll b-buy you a new car," she croaked rawly, but Ty continued to circle the car as if he hadn't heard a word. "I'm s-so sorry..."

And still he didn't hear. The air around him seemed to thunder with muted violence.

Tracy was profoundly sick. Bad temper had

always terrified her. She'd been bullied and manipulated by it all her life. She thought she'd escaped it forever when she'd escaped her mother, but watching Ty now, hearing his low swear words, seeing the evidence of his barely controlled anger, brought back the debilitating fear.

She'd rarely deserved her mother's tantrums. She'd been a good child, an obedient and submissive daughter, pitifully eager to please. But this wasn't her hateful, volatile mother. This was Ty Cameron, and this time, Tracy deserved to be the focus of someone's fury.

The guilt that had strangled the color and energy and hope from her life was twisting her insides with fresh vengeance. Ty had overcome his natural revulsion to help her last night and take her to safety. However much he despised her, he'd rescued her and given her the loan of his car.

Then she'd repaid him by wrecking it and demolishing his garage door before she'd driven the vehicle much more than a dozen feet. She couldn't seem to stop the disastrous course her life was on, and now it looked as if anyone who became involved with her, however casually, would get sucked into her downward spiral.

Despair made her eyes burn. God, she couldn't cry! Ty would surely accuse her of using tears to get sympathy and avoid being held responsible for her mistake. Her mother was an expert at that and

Tracy would die before she'd allow anyone to think she'd do the same.

"So what is it, Tracy?" Ty said then as he glanced across the wreck at her. "Withdrawal from a drug habit or DT's from alcoholism?"

The shocking question conveyed the notion that only an addict or a drunk could have fouled up so completely. That was when Tracy realized she was still shaking wildly. She knew she looked ill and had for weeks. And she couldn't entirely blame Ty for his suspicion. After all, she was secretly terrified she was becoming a drunk.

Since she couldn't truthfully deny a part of his question, she didn't answer, though she took advantage of his attention.

"I—I'm so sorry. I'm not sure how—" She cut herself off and tried to steady the tremor in her soft voice as she fought to withstand the laser sharpness of his gaze. "I'll pay for all the damage—I'll even buy you another car. I'll send a contractor to replace the door, and I'll pay you any amount you set for the trouble and inconvenience this ca-auses."

Ty was as angry with himself as he was with Tracy. All he could think about was that he'd handed his keys and his car to someone incapable of safely operating a motor vehicle. Innocent people could have been seriously injured or killed, and he would have been just as responsible as the woman he'd put behind the wheel.

Ty studied the "woman" who looked as frail and vulnerable as a child. Tracy was shaking, and gray shadows hung heavily beneath huge eyes that were red-rimmed but dry. He saw her mortification and dismay.

And shame. The impression was there again. That and the persistent sense that Tracy was lost.

She'd gotten herself into a colossal mess. First by getting drunk with a rich lowlife like Parker last night, now with this. He'd made some calls this morning and asked around about her. Life wasn't going too well for Tracy LeDeux, however much money she had.

Ty was suddenly certain that if he drove her to town, dropped her at her penthouse and never had another thing to do with her, she'd fall even farther than she already had.

Her softly repeated, "I'm s-sorry. I'll pay for the damage, buy you a new car, whatever amount you say," deepened the eerie sense that he was looking at a woman on the precipice of a swift, devastating, and possibly fatal fall. He wasn't a man who put stock in premonitions, so he couldn't account for the foreboding he felt. On the other hand, it didn't take a crystal ball to see that Tracy was in peril.

Why was that any of his business? She meant

nothing to him. If she wanted to throw her life away, it was her decision. It wasn't his place to intervene.

And yet the compulsion was there. His anger surged up another few notches, then went cosmic when she spoke again, more nervous and anxious than ever.

"I'll pay any amount, Mr. Cameron. Whatever you name, I just want to make it right."

Her desperation seemed pitiful to him suddenly. Then he thought about her wicked, manipulative mother and wondered if this was an act. If it was, he'd soon know.

He held his silence another white-hot moment until she said, "I'll pay anything. Whatever you say."

"You're damned right you'll pay," he growled, hardening his heart as she stared fearfully at him.

Tracy nodded jerkily. "N-name the amount. I don't care how much."

Tracy tried to endure the narrow look he gave her then. She struggled for some scrap of courage, but the stillness about him registered on her as the silence before a blowup.

His tough, "You want to make it right, huh?" made her flinch. He hadn't raised his voice, but her nerves were so ragged that any sound registered like a shout.

She nodded emphatically. "Yes, whatever it takes."

Ty tipped his head back slightly as if to study her from a more precise angle. "Are you a little rich girl who thinks she can just write out a check and fix things when she's careless with someone else's property? And what's the offer of extra payment for, Tracy? What are you really trying to buy?"

Tracy stared at him and felt her horror deepen. "I've a-apologized. Or tried to. I'm really very sorry..." Her voice drifted away as his expression went even harder. "I never dreamed this would happen, but I wasn't careless. I can't explain it, it doesn't make sense. I thought garage doors had that safety feature—" She cut herself off again. Every word she spoke seemed to displease him even more. She was helpless in the face of such unshakable resistance. How he must hate her! "I—I don't know what to say, what to do, I—"

"I know exactly what you can do to make it right with me," he said grimly.

It should have been some relief that Ty was about to tell her how she could fix things with him. It should have been a relief that he was about to spell out a specific course of action that would satisfy him and mollify his anger. Maybe even lessen his hatred of her.

But there was something in his voice and in the arctic blue of his gaze that kept her on guard.

"What do you want from me?"

And still he made her wait. Though it couldn't have been more than a sparse scattering of seconds, it felt like an eternity. When he finally answered, she couldn't comprehend his words at first.

"You work for me, at hourly wages, until the dollar value of the damage is met. The time it takes you to earn enough hourly wages to cover the damage, will be your personal compensation to me for my trouble and inconvenience."

Tracy stared at him as she replayed the words in her mind. He *couldn't* mean that. He wanted her to work for him at an hourly wage until the damage amount was met?

The terror she felt suddenly was overpowering. How many hours would it take to pay off what had to be thousands of dollars worth of damage? And Ty despised her. It didn't take a genius to figure out that he could use every minute of those hundreds of hours to make her life a far deeper hell than it already was. Perhaps doing that to her was what he meant by personal compensation.

Whatever her life had been, whatever it had become, Ty Cameron could finish her off. She couldn't imagine surviving hour upon hour of his animosity and disapproval. And what kind of job was he offering? She had no particular skills or talents, not that a rancher or businessman would value.

A truly sickening and perverse thought came to her then. The memory of Greg Parker—and what he'd wanted to do to her last night—surged back. Surely Ty couldn't be thinking...

No, it wasn't possible. Ty hated her, and surely the loathing he felt for her kept her safe. Besides, he wasn't the kind of man who'd demand anything sexual of her. The thought had only come into her mind because the old fears were preying on her now. Fears that had been stirred up by the events of last night and the terrible reminder of how vulnerable she'd been to a predator like Greg Parker.

Ty's humorless quirk of lips reclaimed her attention. "Have you ever had a job, Tracy? Have you ever learned the value of a dollar?"

Have you ever learned the value of a dollar?

The question stung and brought a swell of black emotion. She absolutely had learned the value of a dollar, but not in any way that Ty Cameron would consider decent or honest. It was her deepest, most devastating secret. If Ty ever found out, he'd look down on her even more than he did already.

But maybe there was a chance—just an infinitesimal chance—that she could make up for one awful thing she'd done. Maybe she could make up for the damage to his car and his garage. If she agreed to work for him and could do a good enough job, maybe he would think a little more highly of her than he did now. Maybe she could redeem herself in his eyes, at least for this one thing.

She didn't let herself think too hard about why it was so important that Ty Cameron stop hating her.

It was a novel idea, this chance to pay for something she'd done wrong with time and hard work. She almost fell for it before common sense squelched the fantasy. Ty Cameron's standards would be impossibly high, probably on purpose. The only thing that was certain was that she'd never be able to meet them, though she'd probably break her heart trying. And when she couldn't please him, he'd break it for her with his scorn and contempt.

That was why she had to refuse. Far better to suffer his scorn now than risk her heart on a hopeless cause that was doomed to fail because Ty Cameron would plan for it to. She tried to sound firm.

"Notify me when you have a dollar amount."

He came right back with, "Does that mean you agree to work for me?"

Tracy could tell nothing from his harsh expression. Cowardice made it hard to speak. It would be so much easier to put him off until she was safely locked at home in San Antonio. She could call him later with her answer. If he reacted badly, she could hang up before he said anything too devastating. Then she could hire a lawyer to intercede for her and persuade Ty to accept her check.

Tracy's gaze faltered as the silence stretched. Terror made her voice small as she struggled for candor. She began to shake again as she dared to make an effort to explain her reason before she officially turned him down.

"What kind of fool would I be to work for a man who can barely stand the sight of me? Whatever you think I am, I haven't quite sunk to the level of asking to be abused."

A bitter slant came to his hard mouth. Tracy could tell she'd offended him. Again. He retaliated, his voice low and quiet, his words painfully on target.

"Sure. Why ask to be abused when you do such a good job of abusing yourself?"

Her heart thudded heavily with the weight of that. Ty nodded toward the Suburban parked in the next space of the four-car garage.

"I'll drive you to San Antonio."

It was that simple. The ordeal was over. Tracy walked shakily to the other vehicle, got in the passenger side, then sat rigidly as Ty got in and started the engine.

The ride to San Antonio was smotheringly silent. By the time they got there, every muscle in her body had knotted painfully with tension.

Ty pulled to the curb in front of her building and she got out. She briefly clung to the door until her legs steadied, then fled to the entrance. The doorman ushered her through and once inside, she hurried to the elevators.

Tracy should have been able to sleep away the rest of the day. Her body ached, her head throbbed, and she couldn't manage more than a couple of crackers on her queasy stomach. She was so exhausted she could barely walk straight, but she was too worked up to sleep. Every moment of the afternoon and early evening passed like hours, until finally she was in her kitchen, facing the small wine rack on the counter.

She'd done everything wrong with Ty Cameron. The memory of those hard blue eyes that had cut and probed and judged wouldn't leave her alone. She should never have borrowed his car, she'd had no business getting behind the wheel. But she'd been so desperate to get away from him that she would have taken any means of escape.

Then she'd compounded all her other "sins" by refusing to work off the damages. It would have been more prudent for her to at least give Ty a chance. Had she judged him too harshly?

That's a laugh, she thought bitterly. The notion

that someone like her would have the nerve to judge Ty Cameron was the very definition of hubris.

It had been a last bit of self-preservation that had made her turn him down. Under the circumstances, she'd made the right choice. Hadn't she? The terrible guilt she felt over the car confused it all and the troubling details of her moral dilemma began another tortuous circuit in her brain.

Tracy began to pace. Again. Wobbly, aching, she wandered the penthouse. If she could make her brain stop replaying it all and analyzing every second of what had happened, maybe she could sleep. If she could sleep and wake rested, maybe she could see it all from a fresh angle. Maybe she'd have some new insight, maybe it all wouldn't seem so terrible. And maybe she wouldn't feel so horribly guilty.

Tracy stopped pacing when she found herself back in the kitchen facing the wine rack. If she could stop torturing herself, if she could fall asleep…

In the end, she knew there was no hope for her. She reached for a bottle and gave in to the inevitable.

Tracy's bathroom was as large as some bedrooms she'd slept in. She loved the large, raised marble platform of the bathtub/Jacuzzi that sat beneath the high wall of windows overlooking the lights of San Antonio. Lush potted plants—some in bloom—rested on the marble tile that skirted the tub. Several hung from ceiling hooks overhead and gave the room the feel of outdoors, though the penthouse thermostat kept it all cozy.

She could lie in the tub of hot, churning water, look out at the lights, and drink her glass of wine. Already the churning water soothed her. The wine bottle sat within reach, the flute of wine was poured, but Tracy hadn't tasted it yet.

There was always a chance that the hot water would do it. The uncommon drowsiness she felt gave her hope, so she waited, trying not to look at the tempting glass or the bottle next to it.

The classical CD that played in the next room was on too low to hear distinctly, but it and the bubbling of the water saved her from silence. She thought she heard the soft chime of her doorbell, but finally dismissed it as imagination.

Tracy didn't know too many people in San Antonio. She'd never invited anyone up, not even Greg, whom she'd arranged to meet in the lobby before their date last night. She'd never got around to hiring a cleaning lady, and when she ate, she went out somewhere or brought home deli food.

Alone in her private sanctuary, Tracy finally managed to focus her mind on the sound of the water and closed her eyes. Her aching body at last began to feel better as her tension eased. Not even the small distant sounds somewhere in the penthouse made much of an impression. Until the muffled sound of what could only be footfalls alerted her.

Someone was walking down the hall!

Drowsiness made her brain slow to react to the danger. Her body felt heavy and resistant as she tried to rouse herself.

The sound of boot heels on tile made her jerk and grab for a towel. Alarmed, she glanced toward the open door and her heart gave a painful jolt.

Ty Cameron stood in the doorway, his handsome face stern, his vivid blue eyes moving over her as if looking for injury. He advanced on her and Tracy fumbled to cover herself with the towel. Its saturated weight made it difficult to unfold beneath the water.

"Get out!" she shrieked as he reached the marble steps to the Jacuzzi platform.

Ty came to a halt, his gaze going to the wine bottle then to the steam that now whited the mirrors and the lower panel of windows.

"You tryin' to drink and drown?"

"Get out!" she cried as she shrank away from him as far as the side of the tub allowed. "H-how dare you come in here like this!"

"You might try answering your phone or the door."

Tracy shook her head adamantly. "You can't come up here without my permission!"

"Your doorman agreed with me. You looked sick earlier and now you don't answer the phone or the door. You coulda been in trouble up here."

"You can see I'm not—get *out!*" she gritted, so desperate for him to leave that she was on the edge of hysteria.

Ty turned as if to go, but instead pulled open the door of the linen closet and got out a dry towel. He tossed it on the tile that skirted the tub.

"Get dried off and find some clothes. I'll be waiting in the living room."

Tracy stared, still shocked by his intrusion. He ordered her around as if he had some right to. He was about to turn away when his gaze caught on the wine flute and bottle. She made a belated move toward both, but Ty leaned over and got them first. His gaze met hers, then dropped to the top of the soaked towel that peeped above the waterline. She could only watch with new horror as his gaze tracked the length of the towel that clung to her body to her thighs.

Tracy couldn't account for the flush of heat that went through her. Or the electric charge that chased it. Just then, she saw something change in Ty's harsh gaze. And suddenly, she was so totally petrified of him that her earlier fears about him seemed minuscule.

Ty's gaze came up to hers and pierced deep. The blue of his eyes seemed to smolder then. *Lust.* It was as if Ty had only this moment noticed she was female. And she was so utterly vulnerable. Naked and trapped, she had only a soaked towel to hide behind. Ty was big and male and powerful. *Unstoppable!*

Her racing heart pounded. *Unstoppable!*

Ty was too big, too strong. He could snap her fragile bones with a careless flick of his hand. He could force on her anything he wanted to. *Unstoppable!*

"Tracy?" The low timbre of Ty's voice was oddly gentle. It somehow penetrated her fear and made her aware that she was shaking wildly. Her eyes felt as huge as saucers.

Ty seemed to see something in her then, something that banished the smoldering heat in his eyes. She saw a glimmer of curiosity, but his expression softened so much that she doubted her eyes almost immediately. Was this a trick to put her at ease, to catch her off guard?

It gave her a new shock to realize that the familiar scorn and condemnation she usually saw when Ty looked at her were also gone. That caught her as much by surprise as his sudden lust. Was she imagining all this, especially the soft look he was giving her now?

But oddly, her fear of him was melting. As he

straightened, his gaze held hers another heartbeat or two before he turned away. He took the wine and the glass and closed the door solidly on his way out.

CHAPTER THREE

TY HELPED himself to a taste from the wine flute. While he did, he walked into Tracy's kitchen, saw the wine rack, and glanced around for the trash can. As he'd suspected, there were two empty wine bottles inside, but little trash besides. A glance into her refrigerator told him there wasn't much to eat. No wonder Tracy was so thin. He put the wine bottle on a shelf and closed the door.

He figured his intrusion might as well be total, so he picked up the kitchen phone extension to call information. He got the number he wanted right away, then punched it in and ordered a delivery. Once he hung up, he carried the wine flute back to the living room and chose a place to sit.

The generous rooms of Tracy's penthouse were immaculate. Everything was decorated in pristine white, with vivid pastel colors here and there, and tasteful wall decor to give it all life and interest. The effect was classy and feminine and more warm than he would have expected with all the white. The huge armchair he settled into was plush and comfortable.

The time it took Tracy to finish in the bathroom and dress seemed long, but Ty wasn't displeased

with the wait. The nagging instinct that had
brought him back to town had annoyed him until
he'd walked into her bathroom and seen the wine
bottle and steamed up windows. People drank too
much and drowned in hot tubs when they either
passed out or fell asleep. It might be the same with
Jacuzzis.

Tracy had been startled and angry those first moments, but then she'd been frightened. And because he knew she'd surely witnessed the lust that
had hit him like a lightning strike, he damned well
knew what had frightened her.

No, not frightened. Terrified. She'd been terrified. He couldn't have mistaken that. Maybe she
was nothing like the promiscuous vamp her mother
was. It surprised him to realize that he hoped Tracy
was as virginal and untouched as she looked.

Tracy fretted over her hair and a light application
of makeup. She didn't pay such rigid attention to
those things to attract men, but to camouflage herself. Though the sleek, shoulder-length pageboy
haircut and the faint enhancement of cosmetics
gave her a natural look, it was somehow a veneer
of concealment and a denial of what had happened
all those years ago.

The khaki slacks and tailored long-sleeved yel-
low blouse she chose looked prim and no-
nonsense, especially since she'd added a belt to the

slacks and buttoned the blouse all the way to the top to help restore her almost obsessive modesty.

A glamorous prude. Her mother called her that and disparaged her for it. But more for being a prude, because whenever Ramona said the word *prude,* the look in her eyes said *hypocrite.*

The reminder almost made her lose her nerve to face Ty again. It was bad enough that he'd brashly walked in on her when she was naked in her bath. Now she had to face him with the memory of this new shame between them.

And fear. Ty Cameron was so domineering. There were no obstacles in life for a man like him, nothing that could stop him if he didn't want to be stopped. Invading her penthouse was proof of that and now her comfortable retreat from the world no longer felt safe.

It shocked her now to remember how safe she'd felt that morning when she'd woke up in his house. The vivid memory slowed her racing heart. And now she realized that although Ty had barged in on her, he hadn't harmed her.

Despite those terrifying moments when she'd seen lust in his eyes, he'd done nothing about it. He'd ordered her around, taken her wine away, but he'd not touched her nor threatened to. She felt a glimmer of trust toward him then that calmed the agitated flutter of her heart even more.

She hadn't answered her phone that day or her

door, and he'd hinted that he'd come here because he'd been concerned. Though she knew he couldn't possibly care that much what happened to her, she was deeply affected. It'd been a long time since anyone had shown a speck of concern for what happened to her. The trick would be to not take his concern seriously.

Tracy again checked her appearance in the mirror, took a steadying breath, then started for the living room to get this over with.

Ty thought Tracy looked as crisp and neatly pressed as a picture out of a fashion magazine. She held herself rigidly and had trouble looking him in the eye when she walked into the living room. She didn't sit down. Instead, she stood behind the sofa that was on the other side of the coffee table from his chair. It was as if she was wary of coming too close and needed to keep a large piece of furniture between them for protection. And that blouse was buttoned up so tight it was a wonder she wasn't choked.

She looked a lot healthier than she had that morning. Her pale skin was flushed from the heat of her bath and maybe from embarrassment. It had been rude and disrespectful for him to walk in on her bath. He'd had reasons that satisfied him, but he doubted prim little Tracy saw it that way.

And that doubt got his attention. He'd discounted Tracy as being as worthless and immoral as her mother, but it amazed him suddenly to realize that he'd judged Tracy so harshly and written her off so completely. Tracy LeDeux was a lot more complicated than he'd expected, and the more time that passed since he'd first seen her in the nightclub last night, the more he sensed it.

"I apologize for walking in on you, Tracy," he began and frowned when her gaze shifted to his then flinched away. "Just so you know, I usually wait for an invitation before I go that far."

The mild sexual reference made her stiffen. "You had no business coming here. I'll have a lawyer contact you about the damage today." As if to underscore her words, her gaze moved to meet his as she said, "If I don't answer your calls or respond when you knock on my door, it means I don't want to see or speak to you."

Tracy watched as Ty's brows went up. "We have business to settle. You seemed eager to make restitution for the wreck, then you refused to meet my conditions. I figured you'd had time to reconsider, so I thought we should talk again."

Tracy lifted her chin. "Is there a reason you have to blackmail people to work for you?"

He took the jibe in stride, but the stern line of his mouth softened. "People like working for me. I pay fair wages and give generous benefits. I value good workers and show my appreciation with cash bonuses from time to time.''

Ty reached into his shirt pocket and pulled out a couple folded papers. ''I got estimates on the car and the garage door this afternoon.''

Tracy eyed the folded papers, then walked reluctantly around the sofa to take them. The dollar amounts listed made her nauseous. Oh, God, so much money. More than she'd thought. She made herself look at him.

''Please...there's no reason I can't write a check to cover this and settle it today.''

Ty was already shaking his head. Now his face was stern again. ''You asked—no, *begged*—to know what would make it right with me. I gave you my answer.''

His tenacity rattled her. It was beyond comprehension. ''I was hysterical and frightened of what you'd do. I don't know how everything got steered away from monetary compensation to—to—indenturement.'' She shook her head. ''Why are you doing this?''

He gave her a searching look. ''Damned if I know. Maybe one of us will figure it out as we go along.'' His gaze sharpened. ''What else are you doing with your life right now, Tracy?''

The question took her by surprise though she shouldn't have been. Ty Cameron meant to have his way, so his question was a means to undermine her reasons for refusing him.

The impulse was to make something up, to make her life seem important and busy. Productive. But as she stared helplessly at him, she suddenly knew he'd sense it if she lied. It occurred to her that Ty'd had a whole day to investigate her life. For a man with his connections and money, it would be simple. And if he hadn't done it yet, something told her he would. She tried a new tack.

"What do you get out of this? Revenge?" She'd tried to provoke him with the bold question, but he took it seriously and his voice was mild and reasonable as he answered.

"Maybe nothing if you refuse to work for me. But if you agree, maybe I'll get a temporary worker to fill in doing small jobs not worth hiring a permanent employee to do."

"It will take months to pay off the damage this way," she argued cautiously, certain he'd given her a way to talk him out of this. "Long enough for you to hire a full-time employee."

Once again, Ty's calm answer was proof of his single-mindedness. "I'm not looking for someone permanent. When the damage amount is met, the job's over. I won't be obliged to keep someone employed, and you can get back to your...life."

Tracy turned away and paced across the room, frustrated. He hadn't said, *You owe me because you took advantage of my trust and goodwill and wrecked my car.* She might have been able to refute that accusation.

But Ty was more crafty than that. He didn't say those words because he could probably tell that guilt was already eating her up. Instead, he made it sound as if her working for him solved a problem for him. She was concentrating so hard on finding a way to counter the subtle tactic that she jumped a little when he spoke.

"You asked me about revenge. Does that mean you think I'll mistreat you if you work for me?"

Tracy hesitated, then turned to look over at him. "You've made no secret of your feelings toward me. How do I know this isn't just a huge opportunity for you to belittle and embarrass me?" She swallowed thickly as his expression started to harden, but she forced herself to go on and verbally acknowledge the thing that was on both their minds.

"I know you despise me because of what I did to Rio and Kane. You probably think I didn't do enough to make it up to them or that I wasn't punished enough, but it might surprise you to know that I agree with you. They let me off easy."

Tracy was shaking so hard that her teeth clicked together a couple times, so she paused long enough to try to control the tremors. Emotion made her eyes burn, but she managed to keep them clear of tears as she said, "I'll never be able to make it up to either of them, but it's not your business to collect on that sin or to punish it."

Just referring to the events of a year ago and saying Rio's and Kane's names aloud sent a sick anxiety twisting through her insides. The guilt she still felt for looking the other way while her mother plotted and schemed against Rio, and for keeping silent when she should have told all, was still as sharp at this moment as it had been a year ago.

Though she'd finally exposed her mother and made certain Kane and Rio got back together, she should have acted weeks before she had. She should have exposed Ramona's machinations the moment she'd learned of them. But a toxic sense of loyalty to her only parent and her deep fear of Ramona's ability to retaliate had kept her silent so long that she'd virtually become her mother's accomplice.

Tracy would never forgive herself for the pain she'd caused Kane and Rio. She couldn't understand how they could forgive her, though they'd both insisted they had and that she was still a member of the Langtry family.

The room dipped abruptly and began to spin. Tracy grabbed awkwardly for the back of a wing chair to catch herself. It was all too much. What had happened last night and today, Ty pressuring her to work off her debt, mentioning Kane and

Rio—even thinking about them and what Ramona could still do to her—was almost more than she could bear.

Ty was at her side in an instant, his hands on her arms, holding her up while she fought her weak knees and tried to force the room to stop spinning.

"How long has it been since you've had something to eat?" he demanded gruffly.

His hands were so warm on her arms, so... *welcome*. The shock of that helped Tracy steady herself. No man's touch was ever truly welcome these days; no man's touch would ever be safe again. Tracy braced her hands against him to maintain a distance.

The heat and hardness of his chest made him seem more big and powerful to her than ever. The solid beat of his heart beneath her palm emphasized the fact that this was a strong, virile, flesh-and-blood male.

Overwhelming. His maleness was overwhelming. And in that frightening moment when Ty's body made an even scarier impression of male power, something faint and undeniably feminine in her responded. *She liked his touch; she liked touching him.*

The fresh shock of that energized her. She pushed away from him and backed up a step. What did this mean? Ty's gaze searched her pale face and she struggled to hide her confusion.

"I asked how long it's been since you had something to eat?"

Tracy shook her head. "I'll get something…later."

"Yeah, you will. I ordered a delivery."

As if saying those words was some kind of magic incantation, the intercom from the lobby chimed. Ty left her to walk to the entry hall and the speaker by the door. Tracy looked on as he answered and gave permission for the delivery to be brought up. Then he took out his wallet and chose two large bills.

He was taking over. Tracy resented it immediately. But there was another part of her—probably too large a part—that felt relief and gratitude that someone had taken enough of an interest in her welfare to intrude like this.

She was faintly ashamed to realize that about herself, but the lonely, lost part of her that believed no one cared if she lived or died, was pitifully grateful. She'd become so immobilized emotionally that perhaps she'd needed someone like Ty Cameron to push into her life and take over a little.

Though she'd known she was in a downward spiral, until that moment she hadn't realized how wretched and needy she'd become. That was also the moment she fully realized she had to do something. Somehow, some way, she had to make an effort.

Ty Cameron was a man who absolutely knew what he wanted and how to get it. Yes, he was domineering, yes he aggressively went after what he wanted. But he probably never had a lonely moment, he'd probably never in his life felt lost. He was utterly sure of himself and convinced of his place in the world. He didn't wake up in the morning and wonder how he'd fill the day. And he'd never have to drink himself to sleep at night because he felt worthless and drowned in guilt.

Tracy admired that, she was hungry for that. To have a purpose, a direction, to have a value to others. To maybe be valuable to herself.

As she watched Ty open her door to the delivery man and easily manage the awkward exchange of food boxes and money, her heart gave a little leap. Perhaps the best thing that had come her way in a long time had presented itself in Ty's garage that morning when she'd demolished his car. As weird as the idea was, the notion that some dark clouds might actually have a silver lining gave her spirits a small lift.

Ty closed the door behind the delivery man and turned with the food. Tracy led the way to the dining room, suddenly worried that she might start hoping. Hope was dangerous because it could be disappointed. Bitterly disappointed.

But as they opened the boxes and set out a splendid supper of Chicken Alfredo and garlic bread on the dining-room table, Tracy realized it was already too late. Hope was making itself felt and the best she could do was restrain it.

She fled briefly to the kitchen for napkins, silverware and glasses, but Ty followed and got the pitcher of iced tea from her refrigerator. At last they sat down to eat and the rich aroma of the food made her mouth water. She offered a quiet, "Thank you," that Ty responded to as he reached for his fork.

"I enjoy Italian food, but rarely get it at home. I figured this might be better tonight than something with a red sauce."

Though he didn't say it outright, he was more than hinting that he'd guessed her jittery stomach might not be able to handle stronger spices well right now. She tried not to let this affect her, either, but if Ty was trying to get her to let down her guard and persuade her that working for him wouldn't be the ordeal she feared, he was succeeding.

The Chicken Alfredo was wonderful. Tracy couldn't remember when she'd last eaten a full meal because food hadn't tasted good to her for months. To suddenly feel ravenous and to thoroughly enjoy a meal was somehow a signal to her that tolerating some of Ty's takeover might not be a such bad thing.

But she was still on guard. When he spoke, she looked over at him.

"Food always tastes better when you've got someone to eat it with."

The remark was another indication that Ty had found out a lot about her and guessed a remarkable number of things besides. Did he pity her? The question was a nudge to her pride.

Ty finished eating. He was leaning back in his chair with the last of his iced tea. "If you agree to work for me, Tracy, and you honestly think I'm unfair to you or impossible to please, you can write out a check and go your way, no hard feelings."

The somber look in his eyes made it impossible to look away from him. She believed him completely and she was wary of that. He went on.

"The work will be hard for you at first. It might be a while before you get yourself built back up and have some stamina. I'm willing to bear with that if you'll do what you can."

Tracy had been about to agree to work for him— on a trial basis—until he said that. She knew of no office job that you needed to be "built back up" to do, or that required physical stamina. Surely he didn't plan for her to work on his ranch?

She shook her head in disbelief. "You don't mean ranch work. Don't you have an office job at one of your companies?"

"I leave the hiring to someone else for that.

Cameron Ranch takes a lot of people to keep it going. There are an endless number of things to do, but you know that.''

Tracy shook her head more emphatically. "I could never do ranch work." And why on earth would he expect it? She couldn't help her suspicion. The best way to guarantee failure was to make her do cowboy work. Maybe he was setting her up for embarrassment after all.

"Why not? You're Sam Langtry's stepdaughter. There's probably not a lot you don't know about ranch work or haven't done on Langtry. Knowing Sam, he would have seen to that."

Tracy plucked her napkin off her lap and rubbed her mouth. She debated what to tell him and how to say it. She couldn't detect any outward sign that this was a setup. For now, she'd be candid about her nonabilities and try to judge his true motives by his reaction. She set her napkin aside.

"Sam taught Rio everything," she told him. "If you think you'll be getting someone like her, you're wrong. I was never allowed to stay on the ranch for long enough periods to learn much. My mother—"

She cut off her reference to Ramona. "Kane taught me to ride and sometimes I got to go along, but…"

Her voice drifted away because she was suddenly reluctant to be quite so candid. She'd been a total incompetent. Rio had been spectacular at everything to do with ranch work or animals. Tracy had often despaired of her own penchant for ineptness, though she'd had only a tiny fraction of Rio's time on Langtry. After all, Rio had grown up there. Ramona had hated the ranch. Tracy had only twice been on Langtry longer than two weeks after the first six months of her mother's marriage, and that second time had been a year ago when Sam died.

But Sam Langtry had loved her anyway. Though Kane was Sam's son, and his foster daughter, Rio, was the daughter he'd always wanted, he'd loved Tracy, too. Sam had probably been the only person in her whole life who'd truly loved and valued her, whether she could do things as well as Rio or not.

But Sam was gone now. And he'd taken everything warm and loving in her life to the grave with him.

"As I said," she emphasized quietly as she looked away from the faint surprise on Ty's face, "don't think I'm like Rio. She was always incredibly good at everything, but I'm...kind of a washout..." She choked off the words *at a lot of things*.

The silence between them pounded her and she stood up to begin clearing their empty plates. She couldn't look to see how Ty had taken her confessions. Ironically, now that she'd decided she'd try working for him, he'd probably changed his mind. Better that he realized it now and just let her write a check. And if he had been thinking seriously of making her do ranch work to humiliate her in some way, maybe he'd decide it wasn't fair to do that to a complete novice.

So what was this strange disappointment, this sense that something in her life might have changed for the better, but now wouldn't? And if he'd been toying with her after all, her disappointment would be compounded. That was when she realized how much she'd hoped he was a good man.

"I'll come to town tomorrow and we'll shop for the clothes you'll need," Ty said then and Tracy looked at him, surprised. Didn't he get it?

"I mean it, Mr.—"

"Ty."

"Ty. I'm not Rio. I'm just about the opposite of Rio." And she was, from her coloring to her abilities. Tracy had always been in awe of Rio and had secretly yearned to be like her. But Rio was too special. Tracy could never live up to Rio's example and it was too late to try.

And if this was a setup, then the knowledge Ty had now about her nonability would make him a bit of a monster if he carried it out.

"If you work for me, then you've already done something Rio hasn't. She turned me down."

He'd worded that like he thought she was jealous and that an agreement to work for him one-upped Rio. "I'm not in competition with Rio," she hastily told him, offended by the idea. "I never was."

"Of course you were," he countered. "It wouldn't have been natural for you not to be, at least a little. But I don't count that against you, so I'll come by tomorrow, say, one o'clock? It'll give you time to have your other things packed for the move to the ranch."

"Move?" She felt the floor shift beneath her feet. Surely she hadn't heard right, but Ty went on with a relentlessness that kept her off-center.

"Your days will start early, probably go late. There are six guest bedrooms at the main house. You can choose one and not spend the rest of your waking hours commuting."

She had to stop this. "I can't do that."

"I'm not insisting on this to get you alone and have my wicked way with you, Tracy. My housekeeper, Maria, also lives at the main house and she knows everything that goes on at the ranch. Probably knows everything that goes on in this part of Texas. You'll like her. And she'll never expect you to make your own bed or wash your own clothes."

His gaze moved over her. "I'd say the first thing she'll do is put some meat on those bones and give me hell for making you work outside."

He set his tea glass aside and stood to help her

clear the table. Tracy couldn't move as she grappled with this new surprise. Ty gave her a handsome smile that took her breath.

"You'll get used to me, Tracy. It won't be all bad." The handsome smile hardened a bit. "I value honesty and good character. If we see eye to eye on those things, the rest of this will work."

Tracy felt her throat close. Somehow she managed what must have passed as a nod of understanding. Somehow she lived through those next minutes as Ty helped her clear the table then left the penthouse.

At least she had an answer to her question about a setup. Ty wasn't the kind of man who'd do that to her, not if he truly valued what he claimed. But his little speech about honesty and good character gave her new doubts about how this would all end up.

After all, honesty and good character were a little tricky for a hypocrite who had as much to hide as she did.

CHAPTER FOUR

THAT next afternoon, Ty was punctual, and his notion of shopping for clothes and ranch gear was a lesson in speed and efficiency.

And he was a tyrant. Her Stetson had to be the *right* one, her heavy work jeans and shirts had to be one size larger than the size that fit her now to allow for a weight gain he'd almost decreed, and she needed boots that wouldn't abuse her feet, boots that had to fit just so over a certain brand of socks that would minimize chafing.

Tracy didn't object. She remembered one of the first times Kane had taken her riding. She'd resisted borrowing clothes and boots from Rio. Instead, over Kane's objection, she'd worn a short-sleeved blouse, designer jeans, and lightweight fashion boots with sheer, knee-high hosiery. Later, she'd hobbled to the house with a sunburn and blisters from her backside to her insteps. The sturdy clothes she'd bought for the ranch after that had been lost during one of those last migrations from Langtry Ranch to her mother's penthouse in Dallas.

So she went along with Ty's dictates. Conversation between them was sparse and her heart was in turmoil from doubt. After buying all these clothes and preparing to move to the ranch, what if it all went wrong? What if she couldn't do the work?

What if she was still totally incompetent, with no sign of improving? How easily frustrated would a man as dynamic and capable as Ty be? Because she was so often frustrated with herself, she couldn't imagine Ty would be any more patient with her than she was.

They were loading the last of her purchases into the back of his Suburban when Ty spoke.

"Having second thoughts?"

The question made her feel transparent. She knew she was good at hiding her thoughts and feelings, so that meant Ty was unusually perceptive. She couldn't decide how good or bad that was, but the fact that he kept doing it made her feel a little as if they had an emotional connection. And that could be dangerous.

She looked over at him. "This has become a big production. It makes me think you expect me to single-handedly rope and brand every head of cattle you own in one morning."

A faint smile tilted his mouth. "Branding season's long past. But if it was the right time of the year, I'd probably let you have a full day."

Tracy studied his face as if she were trying to decide if he meant that or not. "That was a joke,

Tracy." He stepped away from the door and closed it. "You worry a lot, don't you?"

She glanced away from him and he saw her expression go smooth, like ice on a pond.

"Maybe when you get to know me, you'll expect better," he said.

Those large blue eyes swung back to his as if to search for truth, but he ignored her wariness. "You ready to go back to your place and get your things?"

She gave a small nod. "I took everything down to my car this morning. I'll just need to get it from the garage."

Ty stepped forward to the passenger door to open it for her. Tracy moved past him and got in. By the time he came around to the driver's side and got behind the wheel, her expression once again carried a hint of worry. She glanced his way as he started the big vehicle.

"Was your housekeeper there when you took me to your house the other night?"

"Maria took Friday off and she didn't get back to the ranch until after I'd left there to drive you to town. So no, no one at Cameron Ranch—in fact, no one but you and me and Parker—knows you were there, passed-out. But she does know it was you who tore the garage door off and wrecked the car. And before you ask, when you came here with Kane last year, she didn't know why."

He noted the discomfort on Tracy's face. "It's
not the end of the world, Tracy. Take what comfort
you want from the fact that she doesn't know how
you came to be at Cameron and what shape you
were in."

Tracy looked away. "I wasn't drunk that night.
I'd had one drink and only a couple sips of the
second…"

Ty felt a spark of anger that made him ignore
the rest of what she said. Of course she'd been
drunk. It probably didn't take much for a woman
her size, but she'd had enough to pass out. He
didn't like it that she lied about it when they both
knew the truth, but he let it go by. For now.

Tracy didn't select her bedroom at Cameron
Ranch. Maria Sandoz, Ty's housekeeper, had done
it for her. Tracy didn't object. The room was nearer
the center of the house than Ty's master bedroom,
and with an empty guest room between them, it
was far enough away to satisfy her.

She unpacked rapidly, separating out her new
ranch clothes and clipping the tags to prepare them
for a laundering that would soften the fabrics.
Maria returned to the bedroom just as Tracy finished, and over Tracy's objections, whisked the
new clothes away to take care of laundering them
herself.

Ty had asked her to come to the den afterward,

so she went there now. He sat behind his big desk and glanced up when she walked in.

"I'd like you to fill out an application so I'll have something for my records. Then you can fill out your W4."

Tracy came forward to take the papers, but Ty got up. "You can use my chair. When you finish, bring the application to the dining room. Supper will be ready by then."

The meal later began quietly. Tracy felt awkward about the application she'd filled out. Ramona had forbidden her to take any job, and with the fortune Sam Langtry had willed her a year ago, she'd never sought a job after leaving her mother.

She'd had a year of college before Ramona's demands had made her quit. In that year, she'd taken every art class she could because she'd known her time there was short. Ramona had disparaged those, though less vigorously than if Tracy had chosen a more traditional freshman schedule.

It made her uneasy to see Ty read through her application at the table before he set it aside. They were halfway through their meal before he glanced over it a second time. Tracy watched his gaze stop on the area of the form for employment history. He looked up and she glanced at her plate.

"You've never had a job? Or did you leave that

part blank because you don't want me to check with your former employers?''

"I've never had a job," she said, then hazarded a quick glance at him.

"Were you always too rich to have an incentive to work?''

"Maybe so.'' Tracy's gaze fell to her food. No, she and her mother hadn't always been too rich. In fact, she remembered scary times with no money and the ugly schemes her mother had made to get her hands on some. Tracy would never disclose that.

"And only one year of college. Same reason?''

Tracy took a careful breath then gave a noncommittal shrug.

"When you were a kid, what did you want to do when you grew up?'' he asked next. "Didn't you think about one day having a career?''

Now the faint disapproval in his voice was easier to detect. Obviously, he couldn't understand why she'd never had a job or finished college, and he must equate that with laziness or foolishness. Traits that would naturally repel a man like him. His questions made it sound as if she had no ambition at all and no interest in leading a meaningful life.

He would never understand the way she'd grown up or what it had cost her to survive it. Her secret dreams had been submerged beneath the overwhelming distraction of enduring life with her mother. And by the time she'd had the courage and the means to escape that toxic relationship, her dream had been so crushed and disparaged that she rarely pursued it now. And only in secret. It was probably more a fantasy than a realistic dream anyway because she might not have enough talent.

"Tracy? What did you want to do when you grew up?"

Ty's voice called her back and she looked over at him. It struck her that she could tell him the absolute truth because he'd never believe it.

"I wanted to write and illustrate the stories I made up to entertain myself."

It was a huge confession and completely true. And probably sounded frivolous to a macho man like him. His gaze sharpened with interest and she went tense. Would he make fun of her?

She picked up her napkin and escaped contact with his gaze to nervously blot her mouth. Why had she told him? Oh, God, how foolish!

"But I outgrew all that," she said dismissively then set her napkin aside and gripped it.

The pang the lie caused made her feel unfaithful to the little dream, but she'd rather say the words herself than bear up under any hint of scorn from Ty. She shouldn't have exposed something so precious to anyone else. Hadn't her mother taught her anything?

"That's too bad."

Ty's quiet words made her feel restless suddenly. He was simply being polite. He couldn't mean that hint of disappointment. Ty was a man who owned a massive ranch and several companies. Wimpy little dreams like hers were nothing to someone like him.

"What work will I be doing tomorrow?" she asked to get them away from the subject. She managed to look over at him then. He was cutting another piece of steak, but Tracy's appetite was gone.

"I've got a stable hand with a sprained ankle."

Tracy nodded as if that didn't bother her. She'd known that she'd be coming into Ty's job at entry level. But in this case, it would be ground level, since as a stable hand, she'd be shoveling manure and soiled stall bedding. Probably for however many months—or years—it took to work off her debt at stable hand wages.

"Have you calculated how many months it will take to pay for the damage?" she asked.

"Do you really want me to do that?" he replied as he caught the bite of steak with his fork tine and lifted it.

"Perhaps not. But you'll be keeping track?"

"You'll get the pay stubs," he told her.

Tracy shifted her fingers on the napkin as silence settled heavily again. She was going to hate this. Day after day, living and taking her meals under the same roof as Ty Cameron, knowing she could never measure up, knowing that day after day she'd have to face Ty's real cowboys who would think her puny efforts were a joke. Knowing she'd entered a world of strong, capable men where she was too physically vulnerable to ever feel safe.

And all because she'd been lonely and edgy, and had agreed to go out on a date. One of the few dates she'd ever had the courage to go on, and it had led to this.

What had happened that night? She suspected Greg had put something in her drink, but how much time had passed before Ty had somehow found her and brought her to Cameron Ranch? She glanced over at him as he finished his meal and debated how to ask him about it.

The rising anxiety she felt made her afraid of his answer. Physically, she had no indication of rape, but that might not mean anything. Since Greg had surely put something in her drink, he'd probably followed through with the rest. As sickening and abhorrent as the idea was, she was better off knowing.

Perhaps she should have gone to a doctor and been checked, but that might have led to the police involvement that she'd been taught to fear. And there was a chance that nothing had happened. In that case, she'd have put herself through it all for nothing. Her voice sounded choked when she began.

"The other night...how did I end up with you?"

Ty gave her a slow, searching look and her stomach clenched. He must be deciding how to tell her, so that probably meant his answer was as bad as she feared.

She couldn't tolerate the sharp rise of suspense. "Did he leave me in some public place?"

Ty lifted his napkin and tossed it to the table. He looked angry suddenly, and Tracy quailed inwardly.

"You passed out, he carried you out of the nightclub. I caught up with him on the sidewalk and he wisely decided it was best to let me escort you from there."

Tracy's relief was muted by the way he'd put it. But then he went on and her relief was swallowed up by mortification.

"Women like you are a dime a dozen in his life, but he probably wanted one a little more lively than you turned out to be. Once he realized I knew you, he was more than eager to pass you off."

Tracy stared, stung and shamed by his blunt words. She'd thought Ty's hostility toward her had mellowed until this.

"I wasn't drunk," she got out. "I think he put something in my drink."

Ty's brows lifted skeptically. He didn't believe her and that rattled her even more.

"One moment I was fine, then suddenly, I blacked out."

"How often do you have blackouts?"

Tracy shook her head. "No—not a blackout. I've never had one. I just blacked out—fainted."

Ty's harsh look softened fractionally. "There's always a first time, Tracy."

She leaned forward urgently. "No. That's not what this was, I swear it wasn't."

"But you do have a drinking problem." It wasn't a question. And she couldn't deny it because she had too many doubts about it herself.

"I've been drinking some wine at night to help me sleep," she found herself admitting. She exhaled and looked away. "I've been worried..." She forced herself to look at him again, compelled to defend herself somehow. "But I wasn't drunk that night. Even if I'd been comfortable with him, I wouldn't have had much to drink. I only had some of a second drink because he'd ordered it while I was away from the table."

It was difficult to maintain contact with the hard look Ty was giving her. "I've got liquor in the house. Will it be a problem?"

"No. Never."

Ty waited for what seemed like a small eternity before he spoke. "I don't mind social drinking or

I wouldn't have liquor around. But I won't tolerate a drunk in my employ. If you drink during the workday or show up drunk around me anytime, you'll be off this ranch so fast your shadow won't be able to keep up. Got it?''

Tracy felt sick. He still didn't believe her. She gave a shaky nod, cowed by the threat. ''Yes.''

Ty seemed satisfied by that. ''We've got a natural cure for insomnia out here, Tracy. It's called hard work.''

And he had a cure for the small bit of ease she'd felt with him: harshness.

That next morning was a nightmare. Tracy had been too worried to sleep the night before, and after only two hours of cleaning stalls, she was shaking with fatigue. She'd been unwell for weeks, but now she felt so much worse. She was terrified to give in to her queasy stomach and weakening legs, terrified that Ty would have a harsh reaction to any sign from her that could be translated into laziness or an unwillingness to work.

Inexperience alone made her slow, but feeling so sick made it even more difficult to work quickly. And the stable seemed massive. Only a handful of horses were still there, but every stall needed to be cleaned. Which meant wielding a pitchfork and shovel, loading a wheelbarrow with soiled straw and droppings, then pushing it outside to dispose of. She didn't dare slip off to the house for aspirin or Tylenol, so the blinding headache that tormented her raged on.

Eventually, it was only pride and will that made her keep moving. This wasn't just a job to settle a debt, it was a chance for a new start. Her rich life was a shambles that she couldn't seem to fix. As pitiful as it seemed, doing hard, menial labor was so far away from anything she'd ever tried that it might be the only way she could get a grip on herself. However lowly and unglamorous it was, shoveling manure was at least a task she could make progress on.

And that's when the irony of it struck her. That she couldn't spare the energy to laugh only sharpened her determination to go on.

Ty could openly watch Tracy at lunch because she looked oblivious to everything. They ate in the kitchen, but Ty was probably the only one who knew what he was eating and enjoyed it.

At first, Tracy had gone after her food almost desperately. Now she ate as if every forkful was too heavy to lift and once she got a bite to her mouth, she chewed slowly as if chewing her food was too strenuous.

She was sweaty and rumpled, and her hair looked as limp as she did. Except for the deep shadows under her glassy eyes and the bright dots of unnatural color on her cheeks, her face was paper white, and the faint tremor that shook her body was so involuntary that he doubted she was aware of it.

Guilt made it difficult to look at her, but he did. One morning at the stable was clearly far more than Tracy was up to. She didn't just look tired, she looked deeply fatigued. And sick. She wasn't in any condition for this and he shouldn't have pressured her to take the job.

"You can stay in this afternoon," he said, immediately regretting his brusque tone.

Tracy stiffened and looked across the table at him. He saw the delayed focus that came into her tired gaze as it fixed on his face.

"I still have stalls left."

Ty covered his surprise. He hadn't anticipated even a hint of resistance to his order, but there was no mistaking the spark of offended pride in her eyes.

"Someone else will do them."

She shook her head. "You gave me that job to do. If it takes the rest of the day, I'll finish it. I can be faster tomorrow."

Ty heard the emotional quiver in her voice and felt worse. "If you overdo it today, you won't have anything left for tomorrow."

"Yes, I will."

She'd said that too fast, as if she was also afraid

of the condition she'd be in tomorrow but was determined to pretend it wasn't possible. He'd have to be more firm with her.

"I want you to take the rest of the day off. Consider that an order."

Tracy was visibly upset now, putting him more ill-at-ease.

"No. I won't have you say I'm lazy or that I quit easy because I'm too spoiled by my rich, aimless life to shovel a little manure."

"I wouldn't think that at all," he said calmly.

Tracy nodded, but the effort seemed to cost her. "Yes, you would. You already think I'm a lying, dime-a-dozen party girl who can't be trusted around alcohol or other people's property. It's not a big leap for you to think I'm lazy and good for nothing."

She dropped her hand to her lap, got her napkin, and put it on the table. Ty stared at her, stunned. Every move she made was jerky and awkward, but then she tried to stand up too fast and lost her balance.

Ty jumped to his feet and reached across the table to seize her arm as she started to collapse. Tracy's hand shot out to catch the edge of the table, but instead hit the edge of her plate and flipped it to the floor. Ty managed to help keep her upright as he tightly rounded the table and got a firmer grip on her.

Maria bustled into the kitchen. "What is happening?"

Tracy braced her hands against Ty's chest to keep a space between them, but he pushed her down to the chair and forced her to stay there.

"Call the doctor and see if he can get her in now. If not, have him call the emergency room to let them know we're coming."

He was taking over. Again. But even worse, he was overreacting. "No. I don't need a doctor. No emerg—"

"Like hell," he growled and his face was suddenly so close to hers that she could feel his breath and her eyes had trouble focusing. "You're sick. And your skin's hot, like fever."

She shook her head. "I'm just...tired. I didn't sleep well, that's all. I'll feel better in a little while."

"Bull. You'll see a doctor now if I have to carry you there."

Tracy shook her head more urgently, but the room spun and made her feel sick. Still she resisted. "No, you won't. You can't."

He answered that by plucking her off the chair and striding for the door as she struggled weakly to stop him.

"Normally, I admire stubbornness," Ty said to her as he helped her into his Suburban four hours later.

"But not when it puts someone in my employ at risk." He shut the door beside her with a snap and walked around to his side of the vehicle.

They'd spent the afternoon in a cubicle of the emergency room as they waited for a doctor. Tracy had answered the doctor's questions, submitted to a physical exam, then let a technician draw blood for a series of blood tests. Now that the doctor had made a diagnosis, Ty was giving her a mild lecture.

Tracy was too weary to respond. She sat back on the seat and closed her eyes. She was run-down and slightly anemic, with a mild respiratory infection that she thought was a misdiagnosis. The hospital pharmacy had filled a prescription for vitamins and one for antibiotics. The doctor gave orders for only half days of light work activity for the next two weeks—after she had a couple days of complete bed rest. So much for her job.

"You can take me home. I can do the bed rest there," she told him. "Unless you want to forget the job and take my check this time."

"You'll do the bed rest at Cameron where Maria can watch over you."

He started the engine. Tracy opened her eyes and looked his way resentfully. Everything had to be his way. He'd been waiting for her to look at him.

"Unless you'd rather quit."

The way he said the word "quit" rankled.

That's when she saw the tiniest glint in his eyes. He meant to rankle her. He meant to stir her up, to make her too angry to quit.

"So you're not done trying to rehabilitate wayward rich girls. It must give you a lot of self-righteous satisfaction to always have a way to manipulate the people you consider inferior to yourself."

Ty's brows went up and he actually smiled. Another handsome smile that did strange things to her. "Crabby. Mouthy and crabby. That little nap waiting for test results did you some good, didn't it? Another nap before supper should help even more."

The brief spurt of frustration she felt took too much of her restored energy. And there hadn't been much. She looked away from him and closed her eyes. She never knew when they got back to Cameron ranch and Ty carried her into the house to put her to bed.

CHAPTER FIVE

FOR a veteran insomniac, the notion of bed rest was just short of horrifying. Tracy couldn't allow herself to sleep during the day for fear she'd be awake all night. And even if she laid in bed all day and stayed awake, she'd be so sick of bed that she'd toss and turn all night.

So that next morning, she got up early and defied her abused muscles to get dressed and make her bed. She hurried to the dining room for breakfast before Maria could bring her a tray.

Ty was already at the table reading the paper with a first cup of coffee as she came in. His light brows lowered in disapproval.

"You're supposed to be in bed," he said gruffly, his deep voice still rusty from the early hour.

"I can't lay in bed all day and expect to sleep at night. And I feel better." Tracy slipped into the chair at the place that was usually set for her.

He studied her face and she felt uneasy. "You look better. Not feverish."

Tracy took the small opportunity. "I think all I needed was a good night's sleep."

Ty set the paper aside. "You need two days of

bed rest. At least two days, but I'd say more." His gaze was sharp for emphasis. "No argument."

"I'm not sick enough for bed rest," she told him. "In fact, I don't feel sick at all. Just a little sore."

"Tracy—"

"Lying around won't make me stronger."

"We aren't aiming for stronger yet. We're trying to cure exhaustion and anemia," he pointed out sternly.

The "we" of that gave her heart an odd warmth. He'd said it so naturally, as if he had an equal part in restoring her health. Surely he hadn't meant it the way it sounded. He couldn't have.

"I'll eat better, and now I have the vitamins. Besides, what kind of doctor diagnoses a respiratory infection, then tells you to lay in bed for two days? I thought that could cause pneumonia."

"*And,*" he emphasized, "you've got that respiratory infection. The last thing you need is to be out in the dust and hay chaff and animal dander."

Had he changed his mind about her working off the debt? Or was he genuinely determined to protect her in some way?

"I haven't coughed more than once or twice. I think he made a mistake, but even if he's right, I refuse to lay in bed all day. Don't you have something I can do? I realize I might not be up to cleaning stalls, but there must be something. I have a debt to work off. And now there's the hospital bill from yesterday.''

"The hospital bill's my worry, since you work for me. And a few days one way or the other won't matter in the long run.''

"I was sick before you hired me, so the hospital bill's mine. If you already paid it, I want you to add it to what I owe you.''

"Too bad.''

The terse words agitated her. "You're taking over. The hospital bill is my responsibility.''

"You work for me.''

Tracy exhaled, already wearying, but at least she had part of an answer: he still meant for her to work off her debt.

"I'm not one of your horses, so you aren't responsible for around-the-clock care.''

"You collapsed during the workday. End of discussion.''

"I still want something to do,'' she told him then. "Don't you still soap saddles? You have a pool. Don't you need someone to clean it and check the chemicals? There must be something. Otherwise I might as well go back to San Antonio.''

"You're arguing with me now, but you'll go out like a candle in a high wind ten minutes after you get out in the hot air.''

"I won't. I can always come back to the house and...rest."

Maria came in then. "That one should be in bed," she said to Ty as she set two plates of steaming food in front of them. Tracy noted that Maria had brought in food for both of them, so she must have overheard their conversation.

"But, *sí*, she does look better," Maria added as she looked Tracy over thoughtfully. "My cooking will make her strong. Maybe you should let her ride with you, but bring her back to rest before lunch. Then she can stay in and she will not go home."

Ty gave Maria a disgruntled look. "The doctor said bed rest. She wouldn't last an hour, even in the pickup."

"So you both learn something. And you already think she can now last an hour instead of ten minutes. I, too, think the doctor is wrong. She should not lie flat for two days."

As if she knew she'd given as much of her opinion as she dared, Maria bustled back to the kitchen. Ty raised his voice so it would carry after her into the other room.

"Who signs your checks?"

The door swung closed behind Maria, but they both heard her call out with singsong pleasantness, "A very generous employer who is known for his wisdom and handsome looks."

The small giggle slipped out before Tracy could stop it. Ty's disgruntled look focused on her and she struggled to keep the smile off her face. She hadn't expected the exchange between Ty and his housekeeper. Maria's gentle insubordination and Ty's reaction to it softened Tracy's impression of him considerably. The world felt brighter and more hopeful suddenly.

"You should let that smile out," he said then, catching her off guard in a new way. "I don't think I've seen one from you yet. It might be nice." And then he picked up his fork to start eating.

Tracy felt an earthquake somewhere deep inside. One of the first times she and her mother had visited Langtry Ranch before Ramona had married Sam, he'd said something like that. *Miz Tracy, I don't think you've let us see your smile yet. It might be real nice.*

Tracy gripped her fork and tried to suppress the emotion the sudden memory caused. Sometimes she missed Sam Langtry so much she couldn't bear it. She had to remember that Ty was nothing like Sam, nor was he likely to be. Still, as she picked up her fork and ate, she hoped Ty might turn out to have a few of Sam Langtry's special qualities.

Not because she was attracted to Ty Cameron, but because it would mean there might be a few good men in the world.

Tracy went with Ty as he joined his men at the

cookhouse for a review of the day's chores. He'd introduced her to them yesterday, but she'd kept the same low profile then that she did today.

She hadn't anticipated the embarrassment she'd feel at not being given a work assignment until several curious sets of eyes shifted her way. One of the men had probably been given the task of finishing the stable the day before, so by now they all knew she hadn't been able to do the job.

Cleaning out stalls might be one of the simplest, lowliest jobs on Cameron, and probably nobody's favorite, but there wasn't a man among them who couldn't have made short work of it. Which nicked her pride and whetted her determination to have another try at the job.

She was relieved when the men headed out to work, nodding politely to her as they passed. Ty followed and when he paused at the door for her to precede him, she walked out.

"If you still think you're up to it, you and I can take supplies out for a new fence. You can get the gates on the way out and back, but *only* the gates."

It was pitiful how happy she was at being given that much to do. But she also knew this was a small test. Already she felt Ty's gaze on her, searching for any sign of fatigue. And though she didn't feel as rested or eager as she had, she managed to conceal it.

Ty drove the big pickup at a slow speed over

the hard-packed ranch road as the trailer of barbed wire and fence posts followed behind. At each gate near the headquarters, Tracy got out to open it, waited for the truck and trailer to pull through, then closed and secured the gate again. There were five gates before they cut across open range, and that was almost one too many. Already she felt wilted, but the effort to hide it from Ty drained her more.

Frustration made her emotional. What was she doing on Cameron Ranch proving she could open and close gates? Arguing to be given a chore, then running out of steam before they'd gone two miles?

They reached the new fence line a short time later and Tracy made herself perk up. She sensed it the moment before Ty glanced her way, checking again. He pulled the truck to a halt.

"Can you drive a stick shift?"

Tracy looked over at him. "Drive?"

He pointed ahead of them. Two of his men were using the augur attached to the power takeoff of a tractor to drill fence post holes.

"Just drive slow in a line to the left of that tractor, then try to keep it straight from there. I'll drop off the posts one by one, then we'll swing around to bring the trailer back and leave it so they can have the wire."

"You trust me to drive another of your vehicles?"

Ty gave her a mild look and ignored her question. "You can either drive or I'll get someone else to do it."

"But—"

"About the only thing you can hit out here is that tractor up ahead. And that's because the men will probably move too quick for you to run down one of them." Now a faint smile quirked one corner of his mouth.

Tracy was appalled. "Do they all know about your car and the door?"

"What do you think? You're probably the best source of entertainment to come along for any of us in a while."

Tracy looked away and felt her face go hot. She jumped when Ty's big hand closed on her forearm.

"And you're probably the most beautiful woman any of us have ever laid eyes on. Anything you do will attract attention."

Her gaze flew to meet his as a reaction to his touch crackled through her. There was something softer in his eyes, something that made her yearn for things she'd given up on long ago.

He pulled his hand away, but his fingers lingered long enough to suggest reluctance. He took the crackling sensation with him, and Tracy was left with a peculiar ache for more.

Their gazes clung for those next moments and Tracy couldn't seem to look away. It was just a little hard to breathe. She was terrified of a man's touch and had been for years. And yet every time Ty touched her, she'd felt none of the fear and revulsion that was normal for her.

Ty's gaze gentled and she felt a powerful pull of attraction. He got out of the truck then. Still disrupted by those few seconds, Tracy slid over to get behind the wheel as he walked back to the trailer. She watched in the rearview mirror as he climbed onto the trailer bed and pulled his work gloves from his pocket.

Of all the men in the world who might touch her, why was it Ty's touch that felt so good? So welcome? And why did the sudden hope that he might touch her again sometime make her feel a thrill of anticipation?

She'd made it much longer than an hour with Ty that morning, but she was grateful when he brought her back to the house and she took a nap. The heat had stolen her strength. There was some satisfaction in the fact that she'd endured, that she'd managed the clutch pedal smoothly though her legs had gone weak from fatigue long before Ty was finished tossing fence posts off the trailer.

The weariness that finally drove her to bed was an indication that she truly was ill. Later, Maria called her to lunch and she went there still fatigued. Frustration made her feel out-of-sorts, but the good meal left her feeling full and drowsy. She finally went to the living room, chose a large, over-stuffed armchair, then gave in to a nap that lasted almost until supper.

The next two days passed in much the same way. Tracy would ask for and get some minor task that wore her out and sent her, defeated, to sleep the afternoon away. It surprised her that in spite of her worry about insomnia she could still sleep deeply at night.

By the third day, she felt dramatically improved and her melancholy over her lost strength began to lift. She managed to get through the whole day without a nap, but she'd been bored and restless with nothing to do. Maria had finally allowed her to dust the furniture in the living room and the dining room.

Tracy brought up the subject of real work with Ty at supper that night.

"I'd like to try the stable again tomorrow," she told him, then felt injured by the faint annoyance that shadowed his face.

"It's still too much."

"Then why am I here?" she asked, wary of his annoyance but determined to push on. "I'm in the way and I feel even more obligated and in debt to you with every day that goes by."

His stern gaze made her hesitate, but then she dared the small ultimatum. "So I'll go back to San

Antonio until you decide whether you want me to work for you or just write a check.''

Ty set his fork down and leaned back to study her face. ''You aren't up to hard work, but you already demonstrated that you'll push yourself to the point of collapse before you'll stop. If you were well, I'd take that differently. Because you aren't well, it's just a little too self-destructive for my comfort.''

For days he'd been mild with her, gentle. She'd hoped his negative opinion of her was improving, but now she heard the judgment and disapproval in his voice and knew what he really thought of her.

''Why I push myself is none of your business,'' she said quietly. ''You pressured me to come here and work off a debt, so you can either give me a real job as we agreed, or you can take my check.''

''No to both.''

''Fine. I'll go back to San Antonio and call you when I find a doctor who can confirm in writing that I'm able to work.''

She plucked her napkin off her lap, laid it aside, then stood. Ty's blue gaze was fiery and never broke contact with hers until she turned away and walked from the room.

Tracy got all the way to her bedroom before she felt guilty for the exchange. Would every decision she made and every course she took always feel like a mistake? Was she doomed to regret and feel guilty about everything?

She closed herself in the bedroom and leaned back against the door. She'd meant to pack a few of her toiletries and go back to San Antonio, but that suddenly seemed like a tantrum.

Ramona was the master of the calculated tantrum, followed by a dramatic exit. All her life, Tracy had watched her mother manipulate men that way. It made her sick to think she might be like her mother, that her instinct had been to do the same to Ty.

It had seemed reasonable to tell him that she didn't like being beholden to him, to push him to give her work. She was impatient to get on with the job, impatient to feel useful in some way. The mistake had been to push too far, to threaten to go back to San Antonio to find a medical ally to force him to do what she wanted.

Ramona would have done all that and more to get her way. That Ramona would have had a selfish, self-serving motive made little difference. Wasn't Tracy's need to soothe her guilt for something she'd done just as self-serving?

The answer made her feel dismal. She needed to go back to Ty and apologize. As humbling and horrifying as that idea was, she had to do it. Otherwise, she'd be no different than Ramona, who had never in her life apologized for anything and meant it.

Tracy's struggle to not follow in her mother's footsteps was continually thwarted by the fact that she had to sort out the right and wrong of everything that came up, however minor. She couldn't seem to easily find the line between what was reasonable and what wasn't.

Maybe that was what she admired about Ty. He was sure of himself. He had a clear, unbending notion of what honesty and good character were. There was no guesswork for him. Tracy had lived a dishonest life and still did in many ways. Good character was something she aspired to but despaired of ever achieving. Perhaps that was the real reason she'd come to Cameron Ranch. If she could ever measure up to Ty's standards, she'd know she was getting somewhere. The problem was, Ty's standards seemed far too high and demanding for someone like her.

Somehow she gathered the courage to leave the bedroom and search him out.

Ty had seen a flash of Ramona Langtry in her daughter and he'd hated it. He'd walked out to the plank fence along the front drive to cool off in privacy. Cool off being a relative term, since the evening still carried the heat of the day.

The weaned colts in the pasture gradually

ambled closer as he leaned his forearms on the fence, but other than giving out a few pats and a scratch or two, Ty ignored them. He was still thinking about Tracy and whether she was worth a minute of his time, when the colts took note of something in the direction of the main house behind him.

No doubt it was Tracy with her bags packed on her way to her car. The idea riled him all over again, but he was done with her. He'd have Maria pack up whatever she left behind and send it to her. She could get any doctor she wanted to write him a note—if she went that far—because he'd never let her come back. She'd probably go home and write out a check anyway. He'd deposit it in the bank and forget about her.

A picture of Tracy's huge blue eyes and her remarkable face gave him actual pain. Tracy was too troubled for him, too lost. But she was also the first woman to come along since Rio who attracted him.

He understood his feelings for Rio. Beautiful, accomplished and desirable, Rio could have been a full partner in his life. She'd understood his tie to the land because she'd had it, too. But she'd been in love with Kane Langtry.

The feelings he had for Tracy LeDeux were more mysterious. She was the last female in Texas who suited him, but she was somehow becoming the one he wanted. Maybe he'd gone without a woman too long. Tracy was beautiful and aloof enough to present the illusion of a sexual challenge.

And illusion was all it probably was. Touch her once and she'd be all over him. She'd been raised in full sight of her mother's blatant promiscuity. Ramona's marriage to Sam Langtry hadn't slowed her perverted need for sexual conquest. Tracy probably thought that was normal, though he had to admit he'd seen no indication of promiscuity in her behavior.

Was Tracy as pure as she appeared to be or was she a younger version of her mother? The flash of Ramona he'd seen in her earlier only underscored the notion that prim, aloof little Tracy had another side.

The crunch of gravel a few feet away brought the colts to attention. Ty didn't glance back or acknowledge Tracy's approach as he listened to her step off the gravel onto the grass and join him at the fence. Her voice was so quiet he had to strain to hear.

"I've spent my life on the edge of someone else's life. Either no one wanted me around or, if they did, they thought I was too weak or too delicate to be allowed to take part in the interesting things they were doing." She paused. "I'm not offering that as an excuse, but maybe it is. Maybe it's really another manipulation. Like threatening to go home to get you to do what I want. I don't have good judgment about things like that, but I do owe you an apology for doing it. I'm sorry. I'll work when you say or I'll wait. And if you want me to just write out a check and disappear, I'll do that, too.''

Ty glanced over at Tracy, caught off guard by the little speech. He felt a small shaft of warmth somewhere in his chest and caught a fresh glimmer of his mysterious attraction to her.

She was shaking, though she gripped a plank rail of the fence hard to conceal it. She stared out at the pasture, blind to the colts. Her aloof mask was rigidly in place, but he sensed the turbulent emotion behind it.

''You're a hell of a lot of trouble, you know that?'' he asked softly, his own emotions turbulent.

It was the wrong thing to say. Tracy glanced at him then, trying to hide hurt feelings, but failing. He reached to touch her. The impulse was to console her, to reassure her that the remark was the lead-in to accepting her apology and asking her to stay. He hadn't meant to hurt her, but he should have known better.

Tracy shifted before his fingers could connect. Her eyes went huge and he couldn't mistake the fear in them.

''It's all right,'' he said softly, then moved his

hand those extra inches to touch her shoulder. He witnessed the faint flinch then felt her body go more tense as she stayed frozen.

"Wh-what do you want me to do about the job?" she asked quickly. It was clear that she was trying to distract them both from what looked to be sheer terror.

"I want you to stay and rest up a little more before you work for me," he told her, then let her look her fill as she searched his face for the truth of that.

What made her so wary, what put her so on guard that a casual touch affected her like this? He'd noticed it before, but this time it struck him harder than it had those other times. He couldn't account for the strange sympathy he felt or his automatic speculation about the cause.

But then he remembered that day in the truck, when he'd touched her arm and felt a different reaction.

"All right," she said at last, her voice a little breathless. "Thank you."

And then she slipped away from him and walked straight to the house with a rigid dignity that looked a lot like an effort to hold herself together.

CHAPTER SIX

THAT next night, Tracy joined Ty in the dining room for supper. They'd barely started eating when he remarked, "Maria's taking some time off to visit her sister in El Paso."

Tracy's gaze leaped to his. She sensed right away the significance of that and panicked. Without Maria in the house, she and Ty would live there alone, which would be improper. Surely he'd made plans for Maria's replacement, someone who could live in and be a sort of unofficial chaperone, just as Maria was.

His next words distracted her from that worry.

"You're probably strong enough to cook and keep up with the housework. It'll be a good way to ease you into outside work in a couple of weeks."

Tracy stared, horrified. "I can't cook very well," she got out.

"You can read and Maria's got a shelf of cookbooks. I know she's let you do some housework, so you probably know where the supplies are kept."

Now she was completely on the spot. She'd been waiting to work and he'd finally given her a job.

That made it impossible to refuse, whatever her reasons. But what concerned her more than not being able to cook—what absolutely traumatized her—was the possibility that Ty might not plan to bring in someone trustworthy who would live in the house with them.

"You and I would live here…without…?"

Ty's gaze went sharp as he finished the sentence for her. "Without a chaperone?" Tracy gave a slight nod. "Are you worried about your reputation?"

He'd asked that mildly, but the fact that he'd asked at all, that it wasn't a given, was a hint that he considered her reputation too far gone to worry about. The night he'd seen her with Greg Parker and thought he'd brought home a drunk who had blackouts had evidently destroyed her claim to a decent reputation.

She wasn't certain how to handle this. The last thing she wanted was to come straight out and demand that he bring someone else into the house when he'd already decided there was no need. And what would he say if she did? She didn't think she could stand for him to say in so many words that he considered her reputation too worthless to bother with.

"What about your reputation?" she asked quietly.

"I think mine can weather it."

Tracy looked away and made herself get through the meal. What would Ty's men think of her when Maria came back from El Paso and Tracy had to work with them?

A lifetime of shame roared up and she felt the inevitability of failure settle over her like a smothering weight. Ty didn't even suspect the awful secrets she lived with, and yet he'd sensed from the start that she was tainted. He must have.

If her reputation was worth so little to him, there wasn't much she could do to elevate it now. Some things were lost to her forever. Maybe the best she could do at Cameron Ranch was keep to herself, work hard, and try to do a good job. Maybe she could gain some self-respect even if no one else respected her.

It was a dismal way to look at the future, it was a miserable life to feel consigned to. Tracy excused herself and went to her room to figure out how she could suddenly become a fabulous cook.

Breakfast had to be perfect. Everything had to be perfect. The night before, she'd got her car and driven to the Interstate. The huge truck stop restaurant at the junction served hearty food and was open twenty-four hours a day. She'd gone in to read the menu and ask if she could call in orders and pick them up.

Now, at 5:15 a.m., she was slipping into the

ranch kitchen from her first official trip. The small
cooler she lugged in was carefully packed with hot,
cooked food. She hurriedly opened it, removed the
foam food containers, then set the cooler out of the
way in the pantry.

After a quick hand-wash, she got the pancakes,
eggs, fried potatoes, bacon and sausage divided
onto serving plates which she stuck in the micro-
wave for a few moments. She put fresh bread in
the toaster, then filled the insulated server with hot
coffee from the coffeemaker she'd set the timer on
before she'd left the house.

After the toast popped up, she buttered it, then
started taking food into the dining room. Ty was
just walking into the dining room with the newspaper and she gave him a distracted smile before
she rushed back to the kitchen for the rest. At last
she took her place at the table. She noted Ty had
poured coffee for them both.

Her soft, "Thank you," got a quick glance from
Ty as he picked up the meat plate and offered it
to her first. Tracy took the plate, selected what she
wanted, then passed it back. Neither of them spoke,
and Tracy's nervousness began to subside. Ty
didn't remark one way or the other on the meal,
but she suddenly felt faintly uncomfortable.

Though she would never claim that she'd
cooked the food herself, she didn't want to just
announce that she'd bought it at the truck stop. To

her, what was important was that it was good food that Ty liked. Not for anything did she want either of them to be at the mercy of her cooking skills, but the last thing she wanted was for Ty to spurn her rotten cooking and go to the cookhouse to eat with his men. She'd be humiliated if they all found out she was no better in the kitchen than she'd been cleaning the stable.

As long as Ty got his meals on time and she took care of his house, the mechanics of how she accomplished that, even if she was dashing out three times a day to buy cooked food, shouldn't matter.

They finished eating and Ty spoke. "You know how to route the calls from the house?"

"Maria explained that," she told him.

Ty got to his feet, his gaze sharp on her face. "It was a good meal, Tracy. Thank you."

The silence between them seemed to pulse with expectation and Tracy's breath caught. Should she tell him what she'd done?

But then he turned away to leave the house and the moment passed.

Tracy made the calls to the truck stop and the mad dashes to pick up food for the next four days. Getting up at 3:30 a.m. to dress then rush to make the forty-minute drive to the truck stop then the forty-minute dash back, was wearing.

And she felt like a criminal. Ty ate the food she brought, thanked her for it, but the silence that followed made her uneasy. Surely he'd noticed the absence of a cooking process in his kitchen. He regularly passed through there as he went in and out of the house, so he couldn't have overlooked it.

But the silence between them was growing more pronounced. There was always that disturbing moment after he thanked her for the meal when she sensed he expected her to say something. And when she merely nodded to acknowledge his thanks, it was becoming increasingly clear that her silence disappointed him.

And now guilt was eating her alive. The whole issue of the meals had become another tormenting moral dilemma. She suffered it all that day until evening. Supper had gone the same way that all their other meals had, with Ty thanking her for the food, then seeming to wait for something before his gaze went cool and he left the table.

Now he was in the den doing book work. Tracy loitered in the hall, pacing silently nearer the door on the thick carpet, losing her nerve and walking away, but inevitably turning back. She was on another nervous circuit when she heard Ty call out.

"Either come all the way in here and talk to me, or go outside somewhere to pace. Because if that damned floorboard squeaks one more time, I'm gonna pry it up.''

Oh God, he was angry! She'd sensed his bad mood earlier. This was probably the *worst* time for a confessional.

''Come on, Tracy. At least put *one* of us out of your misery,'' he called out next.

She heard the sarcasm in that and resented that Ty could intimidate the hell out of her then chide her for it. She took a steadying breath and walked to the door. She crossed over the threshold and stopped halfway to the desk when Ty looked up and glared at her.

Days of feeling injured over his disregard for her reputation, days of worrying about doing a good job, days of slowly being tortured by his ''thanks'' and his expectant silences all combined to ensure that her bad mood now matched his.

''I took Home Ec in high school and got *A*'s, but the only things I've ever cooked outside of class are eggs, toast, and macaroni and cheese. I love to bake, but you can't live on brownies and soufflés,'' she told him with quiet militancy.

''So I'm not going to ruin your food, then have you go out to the cookhouse and eat with your men. *And* have them know I'm no good at that, either.''

Ty's surly look had mellowed. Tracy was shaking with anger, frustrated by the way she shook like a leaf over any strong emotion she tried to express.

"I never claimed to have cooked that food, nor would I," she said, too agitated to hold back. "You knew I didn't cook it, but I hate that you pushed me to tell you anyway. I especially hate those awful silences and that damned glint of condescending pity I see in your eyes when you give up on me and walk away from the table. It must be gratifying to be so morally superior."

Ty's gaze blazed at the insult, but he leaned back in his chair to calmly study her flushed face. "How much have you spent on the food?"

"It's my money."

"You think I'm that harsh and exacting?"

The question made her more emotional than ever and she gritted her teeth to control it. "Yes."

Ty got slowly to his feet, his gaze gentling on her. Tracy blinked defiantly at the sting in her eyes.

"And another thing," she went on. "I think I ruined your shirt in the wash. I treated it with a stain remover, then forgot to check it again before I put it in the dryer. The heat set the stain permanently, so I'll buy you a new shirt."

"I've got a hundred shirts," Ty said as he came around the desk, his expression somber. Tracy struggled to hold his gaze until he stopped in front of her.

"I apologize for giving you the idea that I'd be

so impossible to please, Tracy." His light brows drew together. "You've really worried about that, haven't you?"

Tracy glanced away and eased back a half-step. His nearness made her feel weak.

"No more truck stop food," he said, and her gaze flashed to his. "You said you can bake, and cook eggs and macaroni, so bake a cake, fry me up a few eggs, then experiment on me with other things. I might even eat macaroni and cheese if you bake me something nice for dessert."

Tracy was already shaking her head. "You work too hard. If the food isn't good—"

"If the food's that bad, I'll drive us over to the truck stop." Now he was smiling, a handsome smile that coaxed her to believe him.

"You're too busy for that. You'll just go to the cookhouse and eat with your men, and then they'll all know what you know, that I'm good for nothing. And then they'll wonder what's really going on, they'll wonder why I'm here. And they'll draw conclusions."

"What kind of conclusions?" Ty's handsome smile had vanished. His expression was hard and intimidating, but Tracy was too upset to stop.

"They'll look at me like men always look at me. They'll wonder if I'm like Ramona. I can't clean a stable, I can't cook a meal, but I live up here with you and Maria's been gone for days."

"So you think they'll conclude that you're working off your debt on your back?"

The blunt words sent a blaze of shame through her that scorched from toes to scalp. Her voice was strangled.

"You told me that you valued honesty and good character, that if we saw eye to eye on those, things would work out. You didn't mention that your high moral standards were conditional, that some of them weren't worth bothering with when you were dealing with certain kinds of people."

The fire in Ty's eyes snapped at the new insult and a faint flush edged his cheekbones. His voice was soft, but there was an edge to it.

"You think there's something sexual between us that needs supervision?"

Horrified, Tracy shook her head and fought against a fresh wave of tremors. "I'm not suggesting that, but I don't want people to speculate."

He was silent so long and his fiery gaze burned into hers so deeply that she felt light-headed. When he finally spoke, she was amazed at how amenable he sounded. At first.

"All right, Tracy. You're probably right. I'll have someone stay here with us at night. Then you and I can relax." His handsome smile eased back, but Tracy sensed something in him that kept her on edge.

His voice lowered. "Because I think there is

something sexual between us. If we don't have to worry about appearances, maybe we wouldn't have to be so vigilant about hiding it.''

Appalled, Tracy got out a breathless, "I'm not interested in...that.''

Ty was close enough that he slowly lifted his hand to touch a skein of fair hair by her jaw. Tracy flinched at the action, but suddenly couldn't move. Silvery tingles moved over her scalp then cascaded over her skin.

Why did his touch glitter through her and make her feel warm and excited? Why was his touch so welcome? She was terrified of Ty Cameron, his size, his strength, his overwhelming maleness. She was so small and powerless against him and she should hate him for being such a terrible threat.

But he made her feel things that were almost as powerful as her fear of him. Maybe she was like her mother after all. Maybe she was man-hungry like Ramona and had never known it before.

Then Ty's hand moved to her cheek and his hard palm settled gently against her skin. His touch made her want more than to feel his warm palm on her cheek. Her body ached softly in places it never had before and the shame of that was that those places were private and sexual, places that she'd never dreamed could ache with anything so nice as desire.

"Please,'' she whispered, broken by the idea

that she could want something even remotely associated with sex from Ty. Or from any man. "Please...don't touch me." The words were barely audible and ended on a small hitch of breath.

"If I thought you meant that, I'd take my hand away," he whispered, and she somehow endured the strange pleasure of his breath gusting against her face. "But you're melting, Tracy. I feel what's going through your body because it's going through mine."

And then his face lowered to hers and her eyes fell shut. His lips touched hers so lightly and warmly that she couldn't pull away, couldn't turn her head.

She felt an odd curiosity, and realized now that she'd felt that same curiosity from the moment she'd bumped against Ty in the nightclub and felt that astonishing charge of electricity when he'd taken hold of her to steady her.

Now Ty's arms eased around her and she stiffened reflexively. Apprehension made her try to move back when he pulled her against him, but the tender force of his mouth stole a bit more of her resistance.

The kiss was a revelation. There was no fear beyond an underlying wariness. Pleasure trickled through her like golden light. She wasn't aware she was responding to his mouth until she felt the cotton of his shirtfront beneath her fingers and her palms slowly slid up the warm fabric to his wide shoulders.

The tip of his tongue touched the soft line of her lips, jolting her. Her restless start made him increase the pressure of the kiss. Suddenly his tongue invaded and she knew a moment of self-conscious surprise as he probed deep and the kiss became devouring.

Fear floated away and she felt herself succumb to the tender aggression of his mouth. There'd been no kisses that time years ago, no expertise, no consideration, no affection. Just a painful, shaming, brutal assault that made her loathe the notion of sex and wonder why the world was so rabid to have something so degrading and disgusting.

Tracy felt no disgust. There was nothing degrading about this kiss that melted her insides and touched her in secret places. A safety and trust she'd never felt before allowed the raw pleasure of his kiss to carry her off.

It was a new shock—and a disappointment—when the pressure of his lips eased and he slowly ended the kiss. If he hadn't been holding her so securely, she couldn't have stood on her own. Even her hands on his shoulders felt weak and unable to grip hard enough to take her weight.

The world was spinning when she first tried to

open her eyes. The rough timbre of Ty's low voice brought everything into sharp focus.

"I reckon that answered a lot of questions, Tracy," he said. "At least for me."

The words caused her the most incredible pain. She pulled her hands from his shoulders to brace them against his chest and push away, but Ty's arms tightened.

"Wait—what do you think I meant by that?" he demanded gently, and Tracy felt a rush of disheartened tears. She could barely speak around the knot in her throat.

"It means you somehow know about me and you've decided to take advantage."

Ty gave her a small shake. "What do you think I know? That you're not very experienced? That you respond like a virgin?"

Shame flooded her like a river of poison. Somehow, he'd guessed about her and put her to the test. Through the bitter filter of shame, she took his words *like a virgin* to mean *like a virgin, but not a virgin,* as if he was letting her know her inexperience was a lame act that hadn't fooled him.

"Don't mock me," she choked, heartsick. "Not every inexperienced woman who's no longer a virgin had a choice."

"Tracy?"

She heard the surprise in his voice, the shock, and the turbulent emotions inside her went still.

She heard her own words replay in her mind, words that spelled out her dark secret almost as clearly as a telegram.

"Tracy?" The gentle rasp of his voice made her eyes sting. She pushed away from him, too confused and shook up by it all to risk a look at his face.

"Leave me alone. I'm not interested in you, I don't welcome…" She shook her head, struggling to make her voice stronger than the hoarse whisper it was. "I don't want anything from you…that way."

Tracy managed to escape then, and she was too distraught to worry about petty things like dignity as she rushed out and all but ran to the privacy of her room.

Like a door she could never quite close, the secret swung wide and crushed her. At first, she couldn't comprehend the reason she'd disclosed it to Ty. The angry, hurt words had burst out before she fully realized what she was saying.

And there'd been no reason to speak them. She'd misunderstood what he'd said and her reaction had come so fast that remembering it made her dizzy with disbelief. Tracy spent most of the evening sitting on the side of the bathtub in her private bath, trying not to be sick.

Though she hadn't disclosed it in so many

words, she'd said too much for Ty not to understand what she'd meant. She wasn't a virgin, but
she'd not had a choice. Her brain shuddered at the
word rape and she hardly ever allowed herself to
even think the word. Now it pounded her head like
a hammer and she could barely focus her eyes
through the pain.

One of her mother's drunken lovers had caught
her off guard and overpowered her. The swiftness
of it still overwhelmed her, the memory of it was
still stark and confusing and devastating. But what
happened later had compounded it all. There'd
been no justice, no one who'd avenged her, though
her attacker had paid in a way that humiliated her
almost as deeply as the violation itself.

It was late before Tracy got a grip on herself.
By midnight she understood why she'd told Ty.
The confession had been spontaneous, borne of her
morbid fear of rejection. It had been instinct to do
that, an instinct to end the strangely tender feelings
she felt toward Ty and this bewildering hunger to
be close to him. If she revealed her ugliest secret,
he would surely reject her immediately, before she
could care for him any more strongly than she already did.

Because she did care for him. She wouldn't call
it love because the word was frightening. But she
liked him, and she was terrified she couldn't stop.

And she loved the way he touched her, as if she

might mean something special to him. Better that he rejected her now before she could love him than later when his rejection would be impossible to survive.

When she finally went out into the bedroom, she fell too deeply asleep to care that she'd crawled into bed fully clothed and curved herself into a tight ball. She was oblivious to the need to get up and figure out how to cook breakfast for the man she might never be able to face again.

The secret to Tracy LeDeux made him gut sick. Ty had rarely in his life felt such deep rage. As he stood beside Tracy's bed and looked down at her, his rage flared higher. She looked so small lying there, so delicate and fragile. Some jerk had taken advantage of that and he was suddenly hot to know who it was and if the punishment had been severe enough.

He reached down and tenderly smoothed a lock of baby fine hair off her pale cheek, then gently ran the back of a finger along her satiny skin. He regretted any harsh word he'd ever spoken to her, he regretted being so tough. He didn't regret that she'd come to Cameron and slept under his roof, but he did regret that he suddenly had no idea what to do with her.

He'd drifted over the line between employer/employee to kiss her. But in truth, they'd never had a real employer/employee relationship, and he knew it would never be that. She knew it, too. It was a situation they'd both danced around, giving lip service to the notion that she worked for him while they both interacted on a private level that was cautiously personal.

Rehabilitating wayward rich girls. Tracy had accused him of that and she'd been dead-on. It also gave him a clue where to take all this. She wasn't really working off a debt, she was trying to get a grip on her life. And now he knew why.

She'd been afraid he'd use the job to humiliate her. She'd been terrified of doing the work with anything less than perfection because she thought he was harsh and exacting. It bothered him that she thought that, but she'd tried to please him anyway.

The tenderness he felt for her now was unlike anything he'd ever felt in his life. And now he was the one who wanted to do everything perfectly.

Ty reached over to pull the edges of the bedspread up and drape it over her carefully before he turned and walked quietly from the room.

CHAPTER SEVEN

THAT next morning, Tracy rushed to the kitchen at eleven-thirty, so upset for sleeping late that she was on the verge of panicky tears. It was bad enough that Ty had ordered her to do her own cooking from now on, she'd missed breakfast and was running late on the start for lunch.

And on top of everything, she had to face him. Oh God, why hadn't she just packed her things and gone back to San Antonio? She'd actually got her suitcases from the closet before she'd felt guilty and put them back.

Now her dread of what he'd say made the idea of a cowardly escape seem almost noble. Surely this was the end, when Ty would glare hatefully at her and order her to leave and never let him see her face again. She had to force herself to take those last few steps to the kitchen.

She walked into the room, then abruptly stopped when she saw Ty standing at the island counter in the work area of the vast kitchen. He was leaning over an open cookbook, his forearms propped on the counter. He didn't look up right away and it gave her a few seconds to brace herself for the awful scene she believed would come next.

Ty's voice was low and mild as he casually paged through the cookbook. "How do you know what this stuff's supposed to look like when they don't have pictures of the finished food?"

Tracy stood rigidly, still braced for a blowup. His mildness sharpened her apprehension. Would he lure her into a false sense of calm then spring a harsh dressing-down on her to make it more traumatizing?

"I overslept," she said, her voice so raw with nerves that it was barely audible. "I'm sorry."

Ty continued to glance through the cookbook. "You were upset last night, Trace. It was probably better for you to get the extra rest."

He was so mellow. And he appeared more intent on the cookbook than he was on her. Tracy moved cautiously closer to the island counter and said, "If you don't mind having lunch a bit later, I can get it started now."

Ty straightened to his full height and she froze inches from the counter. Surely the blowup would come now. He'd never seemed as big and threatening as he did now and Tracy quailed inwardly.

"Are you gonna jump out of your skin if I look at you?" he asked quietly.

The calm question threw her and Tracy stared, her brain scrambling to understand this.

"Not if you only look," she dared shakily. "If you say some—" She cut herself off as he glanced her way and his gaze caught hers. She finished lamely with, "I can't promise."

Ty's gaze was steady and intense, but there was no hint of temper or harshness. And he was so handsome, his bright hair the only hint of boyishness over a stern face and a body as hard and masculine as any she'd ever seen.

"About last night," he said gravely. "I should have come after you and let you know that what you said doesn't matter to me beyond the fact that someone hurt you in a terrible way and I'm sorry for that. You're a beautiful, gentle woman inside and out, and I like you a lot. I don't care that you overslept."

His grave expression eased into a faint smile and Tracy felt her shock deepen. "But I'm gettin' hungry. I vote for the truck stop now and supper here later."

Tracy was still in shock. The silence of the kitchen flowed around them and settled in as they stared at each other, and Tracy grappled to take it all in. Ty finally closed the cookbook and spoke, grave again.

"You know that you and I have something between us that keeps us from being strictly boss and hired hand," he began and Tracy's gaze wavered slightly from his. "I don't know that either of us is ready to put what it is into words yet, and maybe we don't need to. What I would like is a place for friendship in there somewhere.''

Tracy couldn't look at him suddenly. She needed a moment to recover from the fresh surprise of that, to catch her breath. He didn't go on until she could bring her gaze back to his.

''You aren't the woman I first took you for and I'm glad. I'd like you to be more at ease with me and not be so leery of a little temper or a few scowls. I want you to respect me, but I don't have a lot of use for fear.''

Emotion roared up and it was all Tracy could do to keep it off her face. The shaking started and she felt defeated and debilitated by it. Nothing he could have said to her would have been more welcome, but at the same time, his words pulled her over the line between like and love. It surprised her to realize that she believed every word he'd said.

Flustered, she broke contact with the somber sincerity in his eyes and looked away. ''Things don't change just because you say you want them to,'' she said quietly.

''Wanting something is just the starting point, Tracy. What you're willing to do after that to get it proves how serious the want is.''

His words were somehow a promise. The warmth of it impacted her heart and spread gently. She looked over at him and felt a fresh swell of emotion. An engaging smile stole over his lips and she felt her heart respond to the uncommon appeal of it.

"So I'd like to get some lunch now," he said. "You ready to go?"

For one of the rare times in her life, Tracy caught a glimmer of hope. The sudden sense that something in her life would turn out right was foreign, but it lifted her spirits. She couldn't have kept back the small smile of relief that followed.

Tracy's life began to change after that. Things between her and Ty rarely resembled the proper relationship between a boss and hired hand, and for once she wasn't wary or suspicious of the reason as she began to feel the slow growth of friendship.

She hid her worry over the fact that meal preparation that next few days was a joint project, because Ty had decided it would be that way and she wasn't sure enough of him to object. He curtailed his outside work as they looked through Maria's cookbooks and food magazines, selecting meals that were pictured, then organizing the foods and utensils for their complicated forays into meal preparation.

At first, she was embarrassed that she was so incompetent in the kitchen that Ty, who knew far less than she did about cooking, felt compelled to assist. It was later that she realized what he was really doing and her heart was given a poignant twist.

Millionaire oilman/rancher Ty Cameron, who was machismo personified, had humbled himself to work in his own kitchen because there was something about all this—and maybe something about her—that was important to him. He hadn't kissed her again, though they'd come close. Because they worked in each other's space, touches between them became normal and comfortable, though there was nothing normal or comfortable about those swift electric jolts and the tingles of pleasure that seemed to build to the first sexual desire Tracy had ever felt in her life.

Their first efforts to cook together were close to inedible, but they solved that with a trip for groceries that provided them with cold cuts and a variety of junk food to fill in the gaps. By the fifth day, they got the knack, and even Ned James, who had taken up residence in one of the guest rooms, decided he might occasionally like to eat with them rather than go back to the cookhouse to eat with the other men.

On the fifth night, they'd finished supper and cleaned the kitchen, falling into the routine that felt more natural each time. Later, Tracy was restless, so Ty joined her for a walk. They started up the ranch driveway to the highway, the silence between them both comfortable and turbulent.

Comfortable because Tracy felt so much more at ease with him, turbulent because her feelings for him were expanding by the second and she was still wary of what might happen. And what might not.

There was so much he didn't know about her, so much she never wanted him to know. Was it possible to be such a good person that no one would ever suspect the ugliness in her past? Was it possible to be such a good person now that no one would care that she'd been bad once, that her life had been filled with lies and desperate acts? How interested would Ty be in rehabilitating wayward rich girls if he knew all the wayward things she'd done?

The warm evening was sultry and the air was heavy with the smells of earth and sun-scorched grass. Though things were far easier between them than they had been and Tracy was grateful, she was still cautious about what she said to Ty, still wary of how he would take things. When she finally worked up her courage, she glanced his way to automatically check his profile for any inkling of moodiness before she spoke.

"You've made a project of me, haven't you?"

The smiling gaze he sent her carried a glimmer of good humor. "Was thinking of giving Maria another week in El Paso. We might think about offering a cooking show to one of the TV stations.

They could call it, At Home on the Rangetop for Beginning Cooks.''

Tracy laughed at that. "I'm trying to be serious."

He came right back with, "I know you are, but I think you spend more time being serious than you need to."

"The world is serious," she said and felt her smile ease away. "I appreciate what you're doing. I didn't expect any of this."

"I didn't expect it, either, but I like it."

Tracy looked forward and they walked on for a bit before she reorganized her thoughts and worked up the nerve to speak.

"From the first time I met Sam Langtry, he seemed to go out of his way to be nice to me. Looking back, I think he sensed a little of what my growing up had been like, though I doubt very much that it was in him to imagine how it really had been."

Ty's next step brought them closer and his hand brushed hers, but didn't take it. She sensed he was listening intently and waiting for her to go on.

"He was so good to me and he made me feel like finally somebody cared about me. He was this gentle, benevolent father figure, the flesh and blood version of my ideal of what a father should be and I...idolized him."

She sent Ty a self-conscious glance, caught his somber expression, and then looked away.

"My point is that Sam didn't need to go out of his way to help me or do or be anything for me. Just being around a man like him, just seeing how he lived his life helped. So," she said, then hesitated, more self-conscious than ever, "you don't have to go out of your way to be nice to me. You don't have to watch every word you say and every move you make, or carry me around this ranch on a lace pillow because you think I'll break. Being around you and seeing how you live your life helps. I'll try harder to hear what you say rather than what I think you said, and I'll get used to an occasional growl."

"You feel safer?"

Her soft, "Yes," was easy.

"So, you're saying you want me to be myself, growls and temper and all?"

"You don't need to cater to me or my... problems. I understand who you are now and I think I know what you're about."

"Do you trust me?"

She felt his gaze on her and the close scrutiny she sensed made her heart race a little apprehensively. "More than I expected to," she said, a little disheartened that it was still the best she could do. She looked over at him. "I don't mean that as an insult after all you've done these past few days. It's just hard.''

"Just how much do you trust me, Tracy?" he persisted, then zeroed in before she could think how to answer. "You want me to be myself, to not cater to you or your problems, but do you trust me enough to be yourself?"

Tracy looked quickly away, caught by surprise.

"You're still stiff and on guard," he went on. "Less than you were but more than I'd like for you to be. What if you relaxed a little more? What if you let up on yourself?"

Tracy couldn't answer that. Ty reached for her hand and gripped it gently. She didn't flinch and she returned the light pressure as he went on.

"What if you and I just talked to each other? We've been doing better, but neither of us is there yet. So how about this? If you want to know something, you ask. If I want to know something, I ask. If we're upset, we put it in words, argue it out and stay friends. If we're happy about each other, we say it.''

Tracy dared a look at him. Her heart shivered with something that felt like joy as he went on. He was smiling at her now.

"If I say, I'd like a chocolate layer cake with green mint frosting and orange sections for decoration, you can say, 'Tell Maria next week when she gets back.'" His light brows went up as if prompting her to agree.

Tracy couldn't help her smile. "You're really very good at rehabilitating wayward rich girls."

"I don't want this wayward rich girl to give up on me and leave."

The words made her eyes sting and she couldn't look at him. This was too wonderful, too special. She couldn't believe they were talking to each other like this, that Ty was hinting that her approval of him might be as important to him as his approval was to her. If this was a dream, she didn't want to wake up. She didn't let herself think about the things about her he could never approve of, because she needed this moment too much, her soul was starved for it.

That was when she realized that they'd stopped walking, that they'd turned toward each other. Ty slid his hands around her waist. They stared at each other a long moment and Tracy put her hands against his chest. Not to push him away, but to simply touch him.

He slowly lowered his head to hers and his breath gusted against her mouth. "I've wanted to do this for days and now I can't wait."

Tracy's eyes closed automatically and everything in her leaped at the first touch of his lips to hers. Lightly, testingly, teasing, he feathered a short series of faint kisses on her mouth. Tracy felt herself strain for a more satisfying contact. Her hands were on his shoulders and it amazed her that she was pulling him closer. Before self-consciousness could make her stop, his lips pushed forcefully against hers.

The sultry night spun them into a vortex of heat and bright flashes. The kiss was so deep and carnal that she could barely breathe and she was seduced so quickly by it that she didn't care. The whole universe contracted and concentrated to the hot press of their bodies and the wild mating of their mouths. There was no fear, no holding back, no thought of anything but the soul-shaking pleasure and wonder of the contact.

Ty held her up, he must have, because her body was too drugged with sensation and emotion to keep itself upright. She'd never imagined this and could barely comprehend it was happening. It was a long time later before Ty brought the kiss to an end. They stood there together in the twilight, their arms around each other, trying to get their breath back. Tracy's heart was bursting with it all; she didn't know what to do but cling to him and hope it could always be like this.

For the first time in her life, she wasn't terrified by what more there could be. That was the moment that she realized she'd fallen in love with Ty days ago. Every second since then had not only deepened her feeling for him but somehow, without her being conscious of it, she had also begun to trust him in a way she'd never trusted another soul.

The worthlessness she'd felt her whole life began to make an impression then, spoiling the joy. It was inevitable that it would rear its ugly head, inevitable that it would shadow her future as relentlessly as it had her past. How much could a woman like her offer a man like Ty Cameron? If he knew everything about her, would he still kiss her like this? Would he still care if she trusted him or not, would he still want her? If he knew everything, would he ever be able to love her? Suddenly the only terror in her heart was the terror of not being good enough for him.

Tracy clung harder to him, pressing her hot cheek against his warm shirtfront as she tried to hide the desperation that was tearing at her heart.

Ty tried to walk the line between boss and suitor, and managed one of the rare failures of his life.

And he didn't care. Tracy worked for him, first taking care of the house and cooking, then after Maria got back, going with him everywhere outside, filling in on chores. But most everything he had her do was a joint project because he liked to be with her.

She was neither lazy nor incompetent. She was willing to do any task, however menial, but she was rarely confident, though she was so driven to do things well that she always did a fine job.

He was sparing in his praise because he'd quickly learned she mistrusted most of it. So he doled it out like a miser and watched her confidence in herself bloom those rare times he finally made a remark.

The part that excited him most about those next weeks was that she seemed oblivious to the fact that he was courting her. He didn't use flowers and dates, but the less flashy methods of time and proximity. She almost never flinched at his casual touches now, and her wariness of his ranch hands was slowly easing. He doubted she realized she was losing her aloofness and it gave him pleasure to see her begin to relax.

Today they were moving cattle and he had her riding drag. She was a fairly competent rider and it tickled him to watch her deal with one stubborn cow who broke away repeatedly from the back of the gather. Both the cow and Tracy were determined and persistent, but if Tracy could hang on to the sudden turns and lurches of the horse she was on today, no recalcitrant cow would ever stray far.

Tracy followed the small herd, her coiled rope at the ready. For someone who'd spent most of her life indoors, working outside in the heat and dust of the range was surprisingly fun. She'd always seen horseback riding as recreation, so spending a whole morning on a horse was a treat once her body had adjusted to so much riding.

Cattle were another thing altogether. She'd never realized how wily and stubborn they could be. And they were huge, but surprisingly quick for their size and bulk. The cowpony she rode—Arty—was as tough and resilient as a bulldozer, but so surefooted and agile that more than once his maneuvers to outwit a steer had almost landed her on the ground.

The problem cow that had already tried to escape the herd four times was slowing down and drifting to the right side of the gather. Arty must have noted it, too, because his lazy pace picked up and his long stride automatically positioned them farther to the right to shadow the cow.

Two of the other cows at the back began to ease to the left and the moment Tracy glanced at them to judge whether they were planning to separate from the rest, the cow on the right turned fully from the herd to trot away.

Arty took off and the suddenness of it caught her a little off guard, but she stayed on. As if the cow had only been teasing, she gave in quickly when Arty cut her off, then ambled back to the herd.

They reached the new pasture a short time later,

moved the cattle well into it, then regrouped for the return to the headquarters and lunch. There were only four of them, two ranch hands, Ty and her, so the ranch hands rode ahead while Ty and Tracy followed at a slower pace.

"Can you rope?" he asked and Tracy sent him a doubtful look.

He was so handsome, the quintessential Texan, tough and competent. Tracy had a flash of what it felt like to be pressed against all the toughness and competence and felt heat go over her body.

"No matter how many times I tried, I could never lasso anything. None of my loops ever stayed loops," she told him.

Ty nodded. "We'll have to find you some practice. If you're gonna be a cowhand, you gotta use the rope."

The practice Ty mentioned came just before they reached the headquarters. A small bunch of spring calves set aside for a sale were penned in one of the fenced pastures near the south end of a network of corrals.

"Let's see what you're doing wrong," he said, then nodded toward the pasture. "Ride in and pick one. Shake out your rope so Arty knows what you're up to."

They rode to the gate, Ty leaned down to open it so they could ride through. He secured the gate after them and rode at her side as she took out her rope.

Her hands felt awkward as she sorted out the loop and rode toward the nearest calves. They scattered and Arty strode on in calm pursuit, waiting for a signal.

Tracy felt idiotic as she dithered over which calf to go for. She was so self-conscious with Ty watching that she hated to do this without having at least a few practice throws at a fence post.

Ty's amused, "One's as easy to catch as another," prompted her to make a selection.

A half dozen windup swings and she sent the loop flying toward one of the retreating calves. Like magic, her loop sailed through the air and dropped around the calf's neck as neatly and professionally as a seasoned cowhand's.

But the moment the rope made contact, the calf burst into a panicked run. A second later, the rope jerked from her fingers and Tracy watched stupidly as the end of her rope snaked away through the grass with a snap.

Ty came riding up and reined in beside her. After another stunned moment, Tracy looked over at him, her eyes still round with surprise. The slow start of Ty's grin sent heat to her face. Behind them at the corrals, a couple of ranch hands clapped and hooted, sending the heat in her face higher.

"Nice throw," he commented with mock seriousness. "Thought your windup was uneven, but the loop held." The teasing gleam in his eyes made her see the humor in it, but she was still dazed by what had happened.

"I never planned for what you had to do after you got the loop on." She shook her head at the absurdity of that. "I never thought about the other end of the rope."

Ty's smile widened and she suddenly giggled, flushed with the half victory. "But I roped him," she crowed, delighted, "the first throw!"

Ty laughed with her. It was a couple moments before they wound down and Tracy glanced to locate the calf. She saw Ty lean into her peripheral vision and come close. She glanced at him and her breath caught at his nearness as he said in a low drawl, "You've gotta go ask the calf if he'll give your rope back."

"Oh." Tracy sobered a bit and glanced toward the calves. "Yeah." She spotted the one with the rope and was confronted with the new problem of how to get close enough to get it back. She nudged Arty into a walk and tried to find the end of the trailing rope.

CHAPTER EIGHT

TRACY had stepped into a new universe when she'd come to Cameron Ranch. There wasn't a day those next weeks that she wasn't thankful to be there. Ranch work was hard and exhausting, but she felt the nervousness that had plagued her all her life ease, then go away. She gained weight and muscle, and for the first time in her life, she had strong physical stamina.

Being with Ty most of the days and evenings was a wide slice of Heaven. He lived his life with a straightforwardness and practicality that was sane and immensely comforting to her. She'd taken secret note of his habits and the easy way he moved through life and she'd come to feel an uncommon trust in him.

And though she'd now fallen deeply and irrevocably in love with him, the one thing she was still afraid to know for sure or look too hard for was evidence of whether he felt the same way about her. Kisses between them were not frequent, but there was a smoldering tension just below the surface that kept them close. Tracy sensed that Ty held back on purpose, but she tried not to worry about the reason.

She'd needed the solid predictability of a routine of hard work and companionship. She'd needed the stability of a calm emotional environment that had only minor, easily solved disputes, where there was no manipulation or pretense, and she'd found it on Cameron Ranch.

Her past life began to fade in her memory, first blurring at the edges, then eventually fading from awareness. She focused her attention on ranch work, dedicated herself to becoming a better rider, and paid close attention to everything to do with cattle and ranch life. Each day was a test of her stamina and her developing skills. Failures were frequent, but not permanent because she was free to try harder the next time.

Ty was her only real distraction, their deepening relationship giving everything else in her new life a golden glow of excitement and growing peace. The old Tracy would have been wary of so much happiness, afraid it was a setup for another disaster. The new Tracy was too flushed with the satisfaction of small achievements to worry about anything that might spoil the joy of her new life.

It was on a quick visit to her penthouse in San Antonio one day after lunch when she was confronted with the harsh reality of the world beyond Cameron Ranch. She'd gone to check on things and pick up her mail, a ten-minute chore if that, when she heard the doorbell. Though she was surprised she hadn't received a call from the lobby first, she was in too much a hurry to get back to the ranch to worry, and just opened the door.

Ramona LeDeux Langtry stood in the small lobby between Tracy's door and the elevator. Dressed in a crisp white suit that enhanced her blond coloring, Ramona looked rich and elegant and glamorous. Her shaped brow lifted at the surprise on Tracy's face.

"Well, look at you," she exclaimed, then breezed past Tracy before she stopped several steps into the entry hall and turned to scrutinize her daughter. Tracy felt her heart drop to her feet and scrambled to cover her surprise and the sharp dread that clamped on her like an iron trap.

"You look so good," Ramona went on. "Tanned, strong." Her pale eyes narrowed thoughtfully. "Different."

"Hello, Mother."

Her stiff greeting made Ramona smile. "Hello, Mother," she mocked gently. "So very proper. When the way you've avoided me is anything but proper. Or respectful."

Tracy closed the door and leaned back against it, striving for a casualness she would never feel in her mother's presence.

"What brings you to San Antonio?"

"Rumors," Ramona said airily, then turned to walk around the entry hall, glancing over the silk flower arrangement on the long table beneath a gilded mirror. She put out a finger to drag it lightly on the tabletop before she inspected the dust on her fingertip.

"Where are you staying?" Tracy asked then, and Ramona turned to face her with a smile.

"Why, here with my daughter, of course. You certainly have room."

"That's not a good idea," Tracy said, feeling her nerves go taut.

"Why not?" Ramona's lovely face showed faint surprise, but the hard glitter in her eyes pulled Tracy's nerves tighter.

"We can't live together," she said solemnly.

"Of course we can," Ramona assured her with a smile. "We've always been together, you and I. I'll never understand this petty little rebellion of yours the past year, but I gave you a little time on your own."

"I'm nearly twenty-three, Mother. I plan to go on living on my own."

"What about me?" The hint of dismay in Ramona's voice was faked. Tracy heard it as clearly as an alarm buzzer.

"You can go on living on your own," she said, then sent her mother a stern glance to back it up.

Ramona looked injured. "I hardly know what to think, Tracy. Why, you're almost rude to me."

Tracy straightened from the door. Ramona was

about to give her the full treatment and she had to meet her head-on or risk being run over.

"Mother, it's good to see you're well, but I just came back here to pick up a few things. I'm in a hurry."

"Oh? Where are you off to?"

Now the interrogation would begin. And the pursuit. Just like old times.

"Out of town."

Ramona smiled at that. "We can travel together."

"That's not possi—"

"Why ever not?" Ramona cut in, still faking hurt feelings. "My God, Tracy, you were never a cruel child."

The subtle accusation nicked her temper. Her mother's penchant to manipulate her was intolerable. Tracy didn't want to be anywhere near Ramona, and the last time she'd seen her, she'd made it clear. Standing up to Ramona then had been one of the bravest things she'd ever done, before or since, but she should have known Ramona would get over it and keep coming at her. "You know why not."

The faked hurt vanished and Ramona gave her a long, calculating look. "Yes, I do know, dear. You're living with Ty Cameron. Are you sleeping with him?"

Tracy didn't waver. "You need to go, Mother. I want to leave."

"To rush back to him? Does he know about you?" Ramona asked shrewdly. "He doesn't, does he? But you've fallen in love with him, haven't you?"

Tracy didn't answer. Ramona had caught a whiff of opportunity, which was why she'd shown up.

And now Tracy saw that there were more lines on her mother's face and something in the china-blue of her eyes was oddly intense. Though Ramona was still a strikingly beautiful woman, it was obvious to Tracy that her mother had finally started to age. Surely Ramona, who was vain and obsessed with her looks, had detected it.

Perhaps that accounted for the odd intensity in her eyes, perhaps she was worried about her attraction to men. And because she'd amassed several fortunes from men who fancied her looks, she was surely worried that these signs of aging threatened what she'd always referred to as her "marketability."

Ramona's expression went hard and Tracy knew what was coming. It was an old thing between them. When she gave a hint of resistance, Ramona would then began to dismantle her piece by piece until she was too demoralized to fight. A tremor went through her as she fought being yanked back into the nightmare. The pain she felt then was the pain she'd always felt at the knowledge that this beautiful, diabolical woman was the mother who'd given birth to her.

"Well, I must commend you on your taste and your great good luck. Ty Cameron is filthy rich and handsome, but you have to keep in mind that men like him are still looking for that first wife, and his standards are bound to be impossibly high."

"You need to leave," Tracy said with careful calm. "I need to get back."

Ramona ignored the order. "Getting involved with Cameron was a tactical error. And, he's privy to a lot of secrets. He's well-known and liked, very high profile. Your involvement with him is bound to get around, and if he's not properly handled, he can make things known later that could make your next man difficult."

Though Tracy had expected her mother to go for the jugular, she was nevertheless shocked by Ramona's cold-blooded analysis.

"You need to choose an easier man, one who's lonely or one whose ego demands a trophy wife. A man who understands that a woman's been around, one who won't ask too many questions before you make your move."

"I won't listen to this." Tracy reached back for the knob and opened the door. "Goodbye."

Ramona gave a short laugh, but her eyes

glittered harshly. "You can never tell me goodbye and make it stick, Tracy. You know me better than that."

"So you need money." It wasn't a question. Ramona had the ability to fritter her way through astonishing amounts of money, which was why she'd always had schemes to get more.

"Ah, now you're taking off the little white gloves," Ramona said archly. "Of course I need money." Her eyes flashed, and anger began to stiffen her face. "And you owe me a lot. Sam Langtry left you a mountain of money and insulted me with a pittance. You know that wasn't right."

"All right, Ramona," she said quietly, "the gloves are off. No one knows better than me not to give you money and let you get started."

"Afraid I'll never stop bleeding it out of you?" Ramona asked spitefully and the amusement on her face was an indication of how much pride she took in that particular talent. It was also a reminder of one time in particular and Tracy felt the brutal concussion of the memory hit. Spots dotted the air in front of her face and she struggled to make her voice sound steady as she tried not to faint.

"Something like that."

Ramona laughed. "You're very stingy for a girl who has so much to hide."

The injustice of that sent a hot sting of outrage

through her that banished the feeling of faintness. Tracy was shaking now. "Get out."

Ramona gave her a full, genuine smile. "All right, darling, I'll leave. Maybe you need time to think things over, maybe you need to go back to him now and try to decide how he'd take it if he found out everything there is to know about you."

"I won't let you blackmail me," Tracy declared, the softness of her voice a signal of how tightly she controlled her outrage. "You misused a minor child. And since you would be dealing with Ty Cameron, you'd be wise to check the statute of limitations of some of it before you use it to get back at me."

"Yes, you were the shill in a lot of games, darling," Ramona cooed, showing no sign that the threat bothered her. "You always figured them out, eventually, but then you obligingly kept quiet. He won't really care about my part, but he's too principled to tolerate even a hint of participation or consent on your part. And, barring that, once he knows it all, he may object so strenuously to me that he'd never consider having me for an in-law." Her smile widened maliciously.

"Get out." The pain made it difficult to breathe, but she did. In and out, in and out, defying the roaring in her ears and the angry flush that felt as if it was scorching the skin off her face. "I won't let you do this."

Ramona's brows went up. "How do you think you can stop me?" she asked, then started sedately for the door. "Go back to your rich, handsome rancher, Tracy. See if you can decide what he'll think of you—what he'll do—when he finds out."

"Don't ever contact me again, Ramona."

The order made her mother stop and stare her down. "Don't be foolish and don't grandstand with me. I was the only person who ever wanted you and I'll always be all you'll ever have. We're a team you and I, and you're such a beauty now. More beautiful even than I ever was. I accomplished a lot, but together, we'll make that look like practice."

Tracy took her mother's arm then and ushered her through the door. "I never want to see you again."

Ramona pulled her arm free, then turned to smile at her. "We'll be great together, Tracy. Just like old times. I'll be in touch."

Ramona walked to the open elevator, sailed into it, then turned to face her and push the button for the lobby. She sent Tracy a smile as the door hissed closed.

Tracy couldn't move. She lost track of the passage of time as the trauma of the visit hit her full force. Hadn't she known there was a more than even chance that this day would come? Hadn't she known, in spite of these past months, that a future with Ty was impossible, that these months had been a fairy tale, a sweet little dream too fragile to withstand the toxic breath of reality?

She'd blotted those fears from her mind just like she'd blotted out every other painful thought and memory. It amazed her to think she'd been so successful at it, that she'd truly come to believe in clean slates and fresh starts. And that she'd never see her mother again.

Eventually, Tracy gathered her things and left the penthouse, numb. When she pulled her car to a halt near the ranch house on Cameron, she was shocked to realize she had no memory of the long drive from San Antonio.

What if you and I just talked to each other? Ty had asked her that night months ago. And they had just talked. For weeks and weeks and weeks, on nearly everything but the filth in her past. Looking back, Tracy realized she'd only talked about Sam and Kane and Rio, her visits to Langtry, school, and the places she'd been. She'd never disclosed anything but the pleasant things, she rarely mentioned Ramona, never confessed that the things she'd shared with Ty were the only nice things in an ugly life that had been dark and traumatic and filled with fear.

She'd pretended that he'd never need to know because this was her fresh start, her new life, and all the choices to be made from now on were hers alone. But now Ramona had stepped back into her life and showed her who was really in control.

Tracy sat in the car, oblivious to the fact that she'd parked in the sun with the windows up, and that her car was rapidly becoming as hot as an oven. Finally the drop of sweat that streaked down her temple moved quickly enough to make an impression. She lifted her hand, touched the damp streak, then came out of her daze enough to gather her mail and open the door.

She moved like a sleepwalker, then revived a bit when the cool inside the air-conditioned house hit her. She fled quietly to her room and spent the rest of the afternoon sitting on the edge of the bed staring at the wall.

Tracy offered Ty no explanation for her vanishing act after she'd got back from San Antonio, and he didn't ask. The fact that he didn't ask, that he made no demand for an explanation, was a guilty reminder that he trusted her even more than she trusted him, that he trusted her judgment about how she spent her time.

Somehow she got through supper with him, making conversation as normally as possible. Afterward, she escaped to help Maria clear the table and load the dishwasher. Restlessness kept her brain going over everything in a desperate search to cope. Eventually she joined Ty in the den. He stopped doing book work when she came in and she went with him when he suggested they go to the living room to relax.

Tracy was certain that she'd never be able to relax again. Cameron Ranch was no longer a beautiful alternative universe where things were honest and sane. The venom of Ramona's threats had tainted it all and Tracy grieved for the loss.

They'd just settled together on the sofa and Ty had reached for the remote, when Tracy became too restless to stay quiet. She sent him a look she hoped was casual. She even tried a smile.

"Ever think about getting away?"

Ty reached for her hand and pulled it onto his thigh. "Coming up a busy time of year. Fall work," he said, then gave her hand a gentle squeeze. Tracy tried to suppress the faint desperation his answer caused her.

"Nothing too long," she persisted carefully, "just a few days."

If she could get Ty out of range for a while, maybe she could put Ramona off track. If she could wheedle a few days into a couple of weeks, maybe Ramona would get distracted by some other opportunity to tap into money. Tracy was stricken with guilt for the impulse to manipulate Ty.

Ty looked at her then and his gaze sharpened. "You're a little out of breath, Trace. What's goin' on?"

She exhaled a strangled breath and glanced away. It was in her mind to tell him, to tell him now, to confess the parts of her life she'd left out, to risk that they were too close now for it to matter. It was in her mind to tell him, the words were crowding onto her tongue, but the leaden taste of fear and the terror that suddenly twisted her heart paralyzed her will.

Oh God, she hadn't had enough of him yet! She'd loved it here with him, she'd loved him. She hadn't got enough of this rare happiness and contentment, not nearly enough, and her heart was aching with greed for as much as it could stand, for as much as it could get.

"Can't you tell me?" Ty's question was so dead-on—as if he sensed it all—that she jerked her gaze back to the waiting calm in his.

What she said to him was no lie. "I'd like to be with you…someplace. Private."

A slow smile eased over his strong mouth. "Maria's gone for the evening." He released her hand to lift his arm. He settled it over her shoulders and pulled her tighter against his side. "Just how private did you have in mind?"

The heavy sexuality that flowed through her was strong, but even it couldn't ease the sharp anxiety that plagued her.

"I'm not sure."

Ty gave her a solemn look. "You've come such

a long way, Tracy. But as comfortable as you seem to be with me now, as easy as it is for me to touch you, you've never been the one who touches first. You wait for me." He paused and she sensed what was coming. "I've been hoping that sometime you wouldn't wait, that if you wanted to touch me, if you wanted to kiss me, you'd just do it. You have to know by now that I won't refuse. I'd never push you away."

Yes, he would! her heart cried. She hated her past, but a man like Ty Cameron would never be able to live with it. If he knew, he'd push her away in a split second and turn his back on her forever.

How long would she have before Ramona tightened the screws? She'd seen her mother operate dozens of times. Ramona was clever and vicious and heartless. And now she needed money again, probably a lot of it. But she'd also hinted that she wanted them to be a team.

Though Tracy would give her mother neither money nor cooperation, she'd never be able to stop her from retaliating against her refusals. She'd never be able to stop her mother from stealing a future with Ty. The suggestion of getting away for a few days and hoping for a couple of weeks, had been a foolish, fruitless idea doomed to failure, a desperate grab for the last of everything she might ever have with him. Ramona was too tenacious.

"Tracy? Something's wrong, isn't it?"

Desperation made her heart quake and her body go heavy with fear. Ty's question didn't really surprise her. He was so perceptive that he couldn't have missed sensing the emotional avalanche that was crushing her.

"I want to be with you," she said, her voice little more than a choked whisper. "However long you allow."

His brows drew together slightly. "I don't have a time limit in mind, Trace. I'd like for you to stay with me forever. Haven't you figured that out yet?"

Tracy went light-headed. She could see the somber promise in his eyes. Oh God, she had to stop him. She couldn't let him say anything more.

She turned to him then and got up to brace her knee on the sofa. She slid her hands around his neck and before she could let herself think about it, she leaned hard against him and kissed him. The kiss was sudden and it was forceful.

Ty responded just as suddenly and forcefully. In seconds she was beneath him on the sofa, their kisses so lavish and wild that the only sounds in the room came from their ragged breaths, the sounds of cloth chafing cloth and the soft pop of buttons pulled from buttonholes.

She all but cried out when it all suddenly stopped. She opened her eyes to see the reason. Ty stared down at her and his sharp scrutiny made her feel exposed. Her blouse was unbuttoned, the facings parted wide, and now the air felt chilly on her flushed skin. He'd pulled her arms from his neck and his big hands had gently pinned her wrists slightly over her head. His weight on her made it impossible to move.

"I waited weeks for you to reach for me, but I wasn't waiting for that, baby. I love the hot and crazy part, but the desperation isn't the kind I hoped for, is it?"

Tracy flinched and turned her face. The restless move she tried proved she was immobilized. Ty's voice was a gentle rasp.

"I can feel your fear and your eyes are haunted again. What's done this to you?"

The pressure in her chest was strangling her. Tears burned like acid behind her eyes and the effort of keeping them back made it hard to breathe. She bit her lip and tasted blood. The rough growl of his voice almost wrecked the control that made her body tremble with the effort.

"Damn it, Tracy, don't go back to that place you were when you came here. You can't live like that."

The pressure surged and every vein in her body pulsed tightly. Her head swam with the monumental exertion required to keep control. His low drawl battled with the pounding in her ears.

"Come back to me, Tracy. Be here. Nothing back there matters."

A spasm of hard, dry sobs got free and she cried out with the effort to stop them. "Yes, it does."

Ty released one wrist and shifted so his big hand could gently grip her chin and lower jaw to force her to look at him. "Then tell me about it. We'll get it out in the open and look it over."

Her breathless "No," became a series of pained "No, no, no."

Ty's grip tightened fractionally. "Listen to me, Tracy," he ordered softly and waited for her to make eye contact. "Ramona LeDeux left too many men in her wake to have secrets."

The shocking words loosened the tight coil of hysteria she struggled to master. Tracy looked up into his face, fought another series of sobs, then went silent.

"I know a little of it and I can guess more." His fingers tightened again, but caused no pain. "Your conscience is so tender. It just goes around and around and beats you to death over everything, big or little, and it never cuts you slack, even over the things you were tricked or coerced or shamed into, does it?"

The shudder his words caused brought up a strangled sound and a few tears slid over the crumbling emotional dam that held everything back. "I can't...bear—" Her voice broke and she made a restless move. Ty obliged by easing his weight off her. Tracy sat up on the front edge of the sofa then got up shakily to pace. She wrapped her arms tightly around herself, suddenly freezing.

She couldn't face him, but somehow she got out, "You are the most…important person in my life." The admission was a dangerous risk. "Your regard means…everything. I can't bear to tell you, because I can't bear—"

Ty had got to his feet to come up behind her. His strong arms went around her and tightened warmly. "Take a chance on me, Tracy. I won't let you down," he vowed, then pressed a kiss on the shell of her ear.

The tender feelings for him that welled up spread a warm layer of calm over the violent hysteria, but still she couldn't speak. He seemed to know that, so he spoke quietly to her.

"When I was little, my mama used to tell me that secrets are strange creatures," he said softly, and Tracy squeezed her eyes closed, her heart clinging to the gruff timbre of his low voice. "Some are little pieces of happiness and excitement, like when people plan a surprise party for a good friend. Secrets like those have a time limit and they're hard to hold on to because it's easy to get carried away with excitement and let them slip out."

He pressed his cheek warmly against hers and

she gripped his hard forearms. His voice went softer and the turmoil in her heart calmed a little more. ''Some secrets are unhappy ones that one friend keeps for another, but the secret is shared, so the pain is less and its power to torment isn't as strong.''

Oh God, how gentle he was with her. A child couldn't have felt safer, and suddenly she felt like a child, that frightened, lonely child who'd wanted someone to pay attention to her and help her get through it all. Somehow, he was speaking to her as if she still was that child, as if he understood, and Tracy listened closely.

''Some secrets,'' he went on grimly, ''are the bad ones. As bad as they'd be if they were let out, they're worse when you try to hide them. Because this kind doesn't stay quiet in hiding. They've got nothing better to do than cause mischief. After a while, they get mean. They jab you and watch you jump, they lie to you about how bad and important they are, because they like to brag. Finally, some pip-squeak secret convinces you he's some big old monster as big as a house and as deadly as an atom bomb.''

The tears started then, tears that slipped out as easily as a child's. The dimmest memories of her childhood slowly sharpened, and an incredible sadness spread through her and made her feel limp.

''It's something you make up to instruct a kid,

but sometimes adults can find something useful in a little whimsy. The secret of secrets is knowing which ones you keep and which ones are too mean to let fester.''

The effort Ty had made to draw her out touched her and she felt the last of the tension and pressure in her body deflate. It amazed her that a man as big and rugged and macho as Ty Cameron could be so tender, that his compassion for another human being could run so deep that it only enhanced his tough machismo. He was like Sam Langtry in that, but the qualities he shared with her late stepfather were somehow deeper and more profound in him.

She turned in his arms and focused tearfully on his face. She touched his lean cheek then lifted her face to kiss him. There was no sexual passion in it, just a sweet overflow of the love she felt for him and an inability to control the need to express it.

When she eased back and opened her eyes, she saw the gleam of pleasure in his gaze.

''That's the one I was hoping for, Tracy,'' he said gruffly. ''Exactly that one.'' He paused. ''If you'd be more comfortable taking a couple of horses out for an evening ride while we talk, we can do that. Or we can walk. Or we can just stay here.''

He was willing to accommodate her to make it easier, but it was clear that he meant to know everything. The inevitability of it pressed down on her. And maybe he was right. Maybe her secrets had been kept too long. They certainly felt as big as a house, but he was wrong. They were explosive and now nothing would stop them from going off.

CHAPTER NINE

TRACY had rebuttoned her blouse. It was better to be in the house for this. That way, if Ty wanted her to leave later, there wouldn't be the problem of putting the horses up or walking back to the house. She could just gather her things and go.

Ty sat on the sofa, but Tracy was too restless to relax. She sat on the coffee table facing him, her hands gripped together painfully, unable to meet his steady gaze.

"What happened today, Tracy, to work you up like this?"

Tracy's gaze lifted to his then arced away. "Ramona came to the penthouse while I was there. She wants money and she wants me. If you know anything about my mother, you know she almost always gets what she wants."

"Can she get you?"

It was a fair question, but she sensed he already knew the answer to that. "No. Never again," she said, then felt her nervousness ease.

This was it. Whatever happened, however Ty reacted, this one time she'd tell it all. She was so tired of carrying it all inside, so weary of its power over her, so weary of being afraid it would all

152

come out. She'd hated her life, she would never live that way again, and if Ty was half the man she hoped he was—the man she needed him to be—he'd at least know that much.

"Will it help to know that I've found out a lot, that I know your mother's used a lot of men, that she used you?"

Tracy gripped her hands tighter together. "You found out about her, but you probably didn't find out about me, the things I did." She finally managed to meet his gaze and hold it for those next seconds. "I was a liar and a thief, and I was her accomplice. I did what she told me to do and I didn't tell anyone. At first because there was no one to tell. Later because I was ashamed. She was all I had, and I was terrified she'd leave me along a road somewhere or that she'd be arrested and go to jail."

Tracy felt the pressure come back and glanced away restlessly. "You can't know the power of the fear of being even worse off when your life is already a nightmare. And when you believe you're so worthless that your own mother talks about getting rid of you, you try to do everything perfectly even though you're guilty and afraid all the time."

Ty was so still that she almost lost heart. She felt the pressure rise and push harshly against the back of her eyes.

"I was stealing things in jewelry stores and

department stores by the time I was four. A cranky child who has a tantrum and spills a tray of pricey jewelry that a clerk has just taken out of a locked case, is a distraction that annoys people, but it's very effective. If the child is caught with an expensive piece in her hand or her pocket, well, she's only four years old. Too young to understand right and wrong. And her mommy is *so* mortified, *so* apologetic.''

Tracy got up then to pace. "I was the best-dressed little girl in Texas. I wore thrift shop clothes under my coat going into the changing room, but I wore something brand-new and expensive under my coat going out. My job when we were houseguests was to pick through drawers and jewelry boxes while everyone was busy in other rooms. And I was quite a liar, because I had lots of practice pretending ignorance. 'Did I see it? No. What did it look like? It sounds so pretty, can I look at it when you find it?'''

Tracy wrapped her arms around herself and let out a tense breath. "I was on my way to an impressive career as a liar and a thief until I finally had a friend. It was in second grade and her name was Emmy Jean. She didn't mind that I hardly ever talked because she loved to talk. She chattered about anything and everything. I liked to listen because I was fascinated by the fact that she was so fearless and happy.

"One day, someone stole a broken charm from her bracelet that she'd left sitting on her desk. She said she was crying because that charm was special and she was hoping her mommy could get it fixed, but now it was stolen. 'That's why God hates stealing,' she said. 'He hates lying, too, cause both things hurt people and He wants us to be good to others.'"

Tracy paused, her back to Ty. The memory washed over her, bringing with it such a deep sadness that she was silent for a long time.

"When I put the charm back, I dropped it on the floor next to her desk and used my foot to push it against the chair leg to make it look like it had fallen off the desk and Emmy Jean had just overlooked it. But what she said haunted me. I knew there was a God, but I had no idea that He could hate things or that He cared about how we treated other people. I couldn't eat or sleep that whole weekend because I felt so guilty and I thought I would go to Hell. I finally told Ramona that what we'd been doing was wrong and I couldn't do it anymore. But I was standing within arm's reach of her, and she seemed scarier to me than God did that day. I started eating and sleeping again, but I never lost the guilt because the lying and the stealing didn't stop until Ramona figured out how to get richer men."

Impatient with herself, restless and half-sick

with nerves, Tracy started pacing again. "So that sums up childhood. The things with men started and I didn't realize it. It was only after one of Ramona's boyfriends attacked me when I was almost sixteen that I understood she was subtly setting me up. I don't think she meant for the rape to happen, but I'll never be sure. I couldn't tell Sam, I couldn't tell anyone. Ramona convinced me I'd brought it on myself and that Sam's health was too bad to risk telling him. He lived six more years and every day I worried he'd find out."

She paced quicker, but in tighter, shorter distances. "Ramona worked all her blackmail schemes without using me, except one, but I didn't find out about that for a long time. It was related to the attack. If you think about it, you'll know what that scheme was about."

She couldn't bring herself to tell him precisely that Ramona had extorted thousands of dollars from her rapist. Money for silence for four years. Until the day a car crash ended it and the man died.

Now she stopped pacing, exhaled a nervous breath and looked Ty's way. He was leaning forward on the sofa, his forearms resting on his thighs, his hands hanging between his knees, calmly watching her. She could tell nothing from the look in his eyes or his expression, except it was more grim and hard than she'd ever seen.

Perhaps she'd made herself sound too much a

victim. She shouldn't have mentioned Ramona's part in it all, because it deflected some of the blame from her. And she was to blame for what she'd done. A stronger-willed more noble child could have refused to do wrong and faced the harsh consequences. But she'd been too pitiful and terrified to be either strong-willed or noble.

Her voice sounded choked when she found the courage to go on. "But before you start thinking that I was just a helpless victim in all this, I'll tell you something else. When I kept silent about Ramona's scheme to break up Rio and Kane, it wasn't only because I was afraid of her. I think I felt some twisted sense of loyalty to her and I was hoping I could talk her into backing off. After all, she was doing this to Kane, and Kane can be formidable and probably a dangerous enemy.

"But even though it was the thing that finally made me stand up to her and leave, I've come to realize since then that my silence might have had more to do with the fact that I had a mild crush on Kane. He was good to me and though he never touched me, I thought he might be the only man I could ever be with in a sexual way. I was sure he was the only chance I'd ever have for love and a decent family. I had no idea how to make that happen, but Ramona seemed to know how to get him for me."

The lack of reaction from Ty made her look

away. Oh God, she was reprehensible! This had been too shocking for him, she'd given too much detail. About the only thing that was better was that someone finally knew the truth. And now that she'd told Ty, she'd effectively taken away Ramona's means to blackmail her. There was nothing more Ramona could do to her now, because Tracy had done it to herself.

She rubbed nervous palms on her jeans and turned to look out the window into the long shadows of late evening. Remorse roared through her like high tide. She'd said too much. Every silent second that ticked by confirmed it. To be fair, she'd told Ty a lot and it was ugly. Nothing he'd ever experienced in his nice life could have prepared him for this dark little tale and her confession about Kane.

Bitterness swelled through her next and a cynicism she'd rarely felt gripped her battered heart, squeezing cruelly. "So tell me, Ty Cameron, do you still think it's worth your time and effort to rehabilitate wayward rich girls? Or does the task seem overwhelming and useless now?"

The warm, sure feel of Ty's hands closing on her shoulders made her jump. The hard rush of blood in her ears had drowned out the quiet sound of his approach.

"Are you goin' tough on me?" he drawled gently. "Do you think I'm fainthearted, or that I was too naïve to be prepared for this? Or are you just plain terrified? Afraid I'll let you down?''

She pulled away and turned to face him. Her gaze flinched painfully from the tenderness in his. She wrapped her arms around herself and rubbed her hands on her upper arms. "I feel like I'm dying, that I just cut open my own heart and now I'll bleed to death."

Ty moved forward and gripped her shoulders to give her a gentle shake. "What you feel is the hurt bleeding out. Let it go, Tracy. It's over now, done. I'm still here and no one's gonna bleed to death."

That was the moment she finally crumpled. The tears came in a blinding torrent, the sobs tore at her chest, and her knees buckled. Ty picked her up and strode out of the room with her, walking through the house to the privacy of his bedroom.

The shame and guilt of a lifetime flowed out of her until she was senseless, and through it all, Ty sat with her on his lap in his big bedroom armchair in front of the patio doors that looked out on the pool. The setting sun washed over them in a red-gold glow, then faded to indigo, then to full dark.

Like an exhausted child who had cried herself to sleep, Tracy never knew it when Ty got up and carried her to her room. He dragged down the coverlet and sheet, then laid her on the bed to remove her clothes down to her underwear before he pulled the bedclothes up to cover her snugly. He angled a chair next to the bed and sat there long into the night. Once he was certain she wouldn't wake, he got up, leaned to kiss her sleep flushed cheek, then left the room.

Tracy felt groggy that next morning when she woke up. Her eyes were still so swollen from crying that they felt gritty and full. Inside, she felt hollowed out. It was an effort to get up and shower and prepare for the day, but the shower revived her. Running cold water on a washcloth and pressing it to her eyelids diminished the swelling, but she still looked like she'd cried for hours.

It was 7:00 a.m. before she stepped out of her room to start to the kitchen. The house was quiet and the comfortable peace of it seeped deeper into her than ever before. Anxiety stirred at the thought of facing Ty, but it calmed almost instantly. Though she didn't remember how she'd got to bed, she remembered that Ty had held her last night while she'd cried. He'd weathered her life story and he'd stayed with her during the breakdown. Surely that meant they were still at least friends, but even now, she worried that what he'd done had been a simple compassionate act rather than the special demonstration of caring that it had felt like to her.

She stepped into the kitchen just as Ty came in from the patio. His gaze went over her quickly, but she felt the minute search for detail and her anxiety stirred forcefully.

"Are you sure you're ready to be out of bed?" he asked, and the gentle smile he gave her gave her heart a warm rush.

"I overslept. Again." She gripped her hands together in front of her awkwardly.

"We can do whatever you want to today. There are lots of things to see and do around San Antonio." He pulled off his hat and hung it on a wall peg. "We might even get away for a few days, like you mentioned."

"It's a busy time of year," she said to remind him of what he'd said last night. He started toward her.

"I've got good people working for me, we could take a few days if you still want to."

The offer touched her and made her brave. "Are we still…friends?" she whispered, encouraged by this, but wary. He stopped in front of her and reached up to touch her cheek.

"Don't you know me well enough yet to know the answer?"

"I'm afraid." Tracy couldn't help the admission.

"Of what?"

"That this is a dream, that last night didn't happen the way I remember it. That you ordered me out of your house and I'm out there wandering around somewhere, imagining this.''

His face went utterly somber. ''You don't take anything for granted, do you?''

''Not something this good.''

He stepped closer and brought up his other hand. He cradled her face between his hard palms. ''You'll get over that, Trace. Probably just takes time. You'll learn to expect better.''

And then he leaned down to kiss her, softly, gently, but there was no passion, no hint of desire, just a tender expression that warmed her and chased away the lingering chill of fear.

''Maria won't be home until time to fix lunch. I came in to see if you were awake and make you breakfast. Maybe that pepper omelet we made one morning, only this time, I won't argue, I'll use the big peppers.'' He brushed another light quick kiss on her lips to persuade her, then released her to usher her to one of the tall counter stools. ''You can sit back and boss me while I work.''

Once she was seated, he picked up the folded newspaper on the counter and set it in front of her. ''Something interesting in the paper today,'' he told her, then walked to the other side of the counter and got a skillet out of the cabinet to start the omelet.

Tracy glanced down at the newspaper that had been folded to highlight a certain article. Date

Rape Drug Arrest. The words jumped off the page.
She read quickly through the article that chronicled
Gregory Parker III's arrest after five women
charged that he'd used a date rape drug on them.
Ty's voice brought her startled gaze up to meet
his.

"You weren't drunk that night, but I didn't believe you. I didn't even give you the benefit of the
doubt. I'm sorry."

Tracy stared over into his somber expression and
her heart swelled with the deepest love and gratitude she'd ever felt in her life.

Those next days were filled with hard outside
work. Tracy wasn't especially interested in going
off Cameron land, so they didn't go sight-seeing
or take any getaways. Perhaps one day she'd tire
of ranch life, but that was difficult to imagine now.
She reveled in the simplicity of hard work, the
honest challenge of dealing with the stock and developing her physical ability.

Her new life couldn't have been more different
than the old one, and her growing sense of purpose
and slowly building self-confidence settled her
somehow and gave her a clear sense of direction
and stability. She rarely thought about Ramona
those next days, and she kept too busy for anxiety
about her threats.

Tracy's admiration for Ty soared. There was a

new closeness between them and an understanding and trust that needed no more complicated expression than a look or a warm touch. Tracy felt a remarkable inner freedom that made it easy to touch him first and wonderful to sometimes take the initiative for a kiss or an embrace.

The level of sensuality between them deepened and became intense, but the fact that there was always a careful limit was faintly troubling to her. She was ready for more and she trusted Ty for what happened next, but it was the one subject she couldn't mention, the one thing between them that she couldn't put to a test.

She hoped it was because Ty was old-fashioned enough to wait for marriage, which she preferred, but then, he was a sexually experienced man. She worried that he held back because he was too careful of her past to become intimate with her when he had no intention to marry her.

The dark seed Ramona had planted, that Ty's standards for a first wife would be impossibly high, caused the only ripple in the steady calm of those next days.

Eventually, Tracy realized that whatever became of her relationship with Ty, he'd already given her more than she'd ever hoped to have. Thanks to him, her life had changed in monumental ways. If nothing else, his friendship and care had made her strong. For her, there'd be no going back. She'd never again be that fragile lost soul on the verge of self-destruction she'd been when she'd first come to Cameron Ranch.

Whatever happened, she had her new start and she'd blossomed. If she someday had to leave Ty and this peaceful place, she'd do it and she'd go on as the better person she was now. She'd find a new place and a new purpose and she'd live the best life she knew how. She'd remember all this with great fondness as the special opportunity a kind, decent man had once given her, and value it always as the one part of her life she'd never regret or feel shame for.

But each of those next nights she laid in her bed and prayed it would all come right, that she'd never have to find the kind of courage and strength it would take to walk away from Ty Cameron.

The hot Texas afternoon was bright and scorching, but Tracy had adjusted to the heat remarkably well. She and Ty were out at the shaded corrals doctoring a barbed wire cut on one of the colts. The colt was jumpy and in pain, and it had taken patience and quick skill for Ty to stitch the chest wound once the anesthetic had taken effect. Tracy held the twitch that they'd secured around the youngster's upper lip to distract and control him. The colt had submitted, but grew restless again by the time Ty finished and efficiently administered a shot of antibiotics.

At his nod, Tracy released the twitch then gave the colt a calming rub. The colt fidgeted and tossed his head, but he didn't pull back as Tracy held on to his halter and spoke soothingly to him. He responded to her and calmed a bit, and Tracy finally let him go as a gentle reward. The colt stayed close to her and followed companionably as she started for the gate.

"You've got a nice touch, Tracy," Ty remarked as they walked. The spark of humor in his voice was a clue. "And the colts seem to like it, too."

Tracy sent him a chiding glance, but the cell phone Ty had left on the gate trilled lightly to distract them. Ty was waiting for an important call, and this might be it. Tracy took the small medical kit he handed over, then took care of opening and closing the gate as they walked through and Ty listened to the caller.

She was so attuned to his moods now that she sensed his grimness instantly and looked at him. Anger glittered darkly in his blue gaze, but he ended the call with a terse, "We're on our way," before he looked at her. He hesitated long enough to touch her arm.

"Ramona's at the house, asking to see you."

Thoughts of Ramona were so far from her mind that day that at first it seemed odd to hear her name. The idea that Ramona had come to the ranch seemed unreal, but the sharp dig of anxiety was real enough.

"Then this is it," she said grimly, resolved to facing Ramona down.

"I'd like to be there," he told her and she could tell by his hard expression that it wasn't really a request. Tracy glanced away, undecided.

"You know how we work cattle," he said then, and the apparent switch in subject surprised her, but he went on. "We get a rope on 'em and drag 'em away from the others, then we work 'em over. Ramona woulda made an ace cowhand."

Tracy gave a faint smile and nodded. "You're right. That's the way she operates. And then she sends you back to the herd wondering what happened."

Ty turned her to face him fully. She lifted her hands to his chest.

"Listen to me, Tracy, because I want to say this ahead of time. There's nothing she can think of to tell, nothing she can make up that will make a bit of difference in what I feel for you. You need to know that because I want to be there with you this time. Not because I think you can't handle it, but because I want to see the woman I care about finally close the door on a dark time in her life. And when Ramona understands that nothing she can try worries either of us, she'll realize she wasted the trip out here.''

Tracy stared at his shirtfront and tried to control the emotion his words caused her. ''It might get ugly and profane.''

He lifted her chin with the side of a finger. ''Ugly and profane don't bother me, Trace. We'll see the last of them today.''

She rubbed his shirtfront, overcome for a moment as she considered how good it would be to face Ramona with someone to stand by her.

''Come on, darlin','' he drawled. ''We do everything else around here together. We're good at it.'' Tracy looked up at him as he said, ''We're good together.''

''Yes,'' she said softly. ''We are good together, aren't we? You're good for me.''

Ty turned then and pulled her against his side. Tracy put her arm around his lean middle and they walked together up the alley that bisected the corrals, then through the barn toward the main house.

CHAPTER TEN

THE tension that made Tracy's nerves go taut was strong, but reasonable under the circumstances. She didn't struggle to prepare for this sudden meeting with Ramona because she realized she didn't need to scrape up her courage. The self-confidence that had been building since she'd come to Cameron—since she'd confided in Ty and hadn't been rejected—was suddenly strong.

She'd faced the most traumatizing events of her life alone and she'd been debilitated by fear. This time, she wasn't alone and because she'd come so far, she was no longer afraid of Ramona. Suddenly she knew that this meeting with her mother would go well. It would be difficult, yes, but nothing more.

The sense she had—that this was the last time she'd have to deal with Ramona—gave her a momentary pang. After all, Ramona was her mother. But the faint excitement she began to feel, the taste of new freedom, was far stronger.

By the time they walked into the kitchen, Tracy felt a deep calm that banished any hint of anxiety. She was ready for Ramona and eager to be done with it all.

The unguarded start of surprise that Ramona showed when Tracy walked into the living room was proof that her outward calm appeared as clear and unshakable to Ramona as it felt. Ramona recovered quickly, then flicked an assessing glance over Ty, who followed Tracy in.

"Hello, Mr. Cameron, how nice to see you again," Ramona said, then smiled and settled back more comfortably in the wing chair she'd chosen. She got directly down to business. "I was hoping to visit my daughter alone for a while. Would you mind?"

Tracy leaned a hip casually against the side of the sofa back. "I mind, Ramona. I didn't plan for you to be here long. And there's nothing you and I can 'visit' about that Mr. Cameron can't hear."

Though Tracy didn't sit, Ty did, selecting the overstuffed chair at the far end of the coffee table. He tossed his hat to the empty sofa, lifted his boots to the tabletop and crossed his ankles to make himself comfortable.

Something about that seemed to make Ramona edgy, but she smiled and linked her fingers together over her lap to cover it.

"But, darling," she wheedled sweetly, sending Tracy a meaningful glance, "I don't think Mr. Cam—"

"There are only two subjects you and I could 'visit' about," Tracy cut in briskly, "and I'll settle both of them now. I won't give you money and I don't care to see you again."

Tracy felt the shock wave as her blunt words impacted Ramona. Perhaps she was rushing this, but she suddenly couldn't tolerate giving Ramona a chance to toy with her. She'd had enough to last a lifetime. Several lifetimes.

Ramona found her voice and bristled with careful outrage. "How dare you speak to your mother in that manner, Tracy." As if she realized that she was still sitting, and therefore in a subordinate posture, Ramona stood.

"How dare you come here to blackmail your daughter," Tracy returned easily. "Your only child."

Ramona's face showed a hint of confusion before her light brows went up. "My, my, how do you account for this…brave show?" Ramona pretended to study her a moment. "You seem very confident." She glanced briefly at Ty as if to remind Tracy that he was still there. "Very confident. In yourself and in Mr. Cameron. I can't imagine how that could be, not under the circumstances."

"Mr. Cameron knows everything there is to know, Ramona. There are no secrets between us, nothing for you to use. You'll have to go away and work this scheme on someone with more to hide than you do."

"You told him everything?" Ramona asked doubtfully, her haughty, raised brow expression so calculated that she suddenly looked like an amateur actor in a bad play.

Tracy saw then how pitiful Ramona was. She'd plotted and schemed her whole life to get her hands on more, to better her circumstances by exploiting others and using them to get money. She might have used her shrewdness and intelligence to make something good of her life, but for reasons that Tracy would never understand, she'd chosen the life of a criminal. A criminal wily enough to have never been caught, but no less a criminal.

"Everything, Ramona," Tracy repeated. "You need to leave now."

Quick fury mottled her mother's face and thinned her lips. "He doesn't know everything," she scoffed recklessly. "You're too weak to have told him everything. And even if you were brave enough, you're too worried about what people think of you to have the guts to confess to him or anyone else that you were the highest paid whore in Texas."

The shocking words were no less than Tracy had expected. And she didn't glance at Ty to see their impact. "It's hard to believe you've just disclosed what you must have thought was your most powerful bargaining chip, Ramona. You must be losing the knack. Ty knows about the man you extorted money from to keep silent about the rape. I think legally it would be called witness tampering, because what was done to me was a crime that should have been reported and prosecuted. Instead, you bullied me into silence and extorted money from my rapist. I don't know if there's a statute of limitations on any of that in this state, but I'm sure I could find out."

Ramona was rattled by her gaffe, and she scrambled to recover. "You'd never expose any of that to the press to get back at me."

"All I want is to get you out of my life, Ramona, and I mean for it to be permanent. So it wouldn't be the press I'd notify, it would be the police. If I were you, I don't think I'd be comfortable having them poke around in my past. There's quite a long list of names they could be provided with. And attorneys cost lots of money, particularly the criminal ones."

"You little bitch!" Ramona cried and advanced on her.

Tracy heard Ty's feet hit the floor and felt it when he surged to his feet to intervene. She gave her mother a warning glare that brought Ramona to a sudden stop. Tracy saw the uncertainty in the other woman, and felt the victory at last.

"That was wise," Tracy commented softly. "You really do need to leave now."

And that was all it took. Ramona stared hatefully

at her a handful of long, tense moments, then turned away to grab up her handbag. She stalked from the room and Tracy followed at a distance to make sure she went out the door. She watched from the front windows of the foyer as Ramona marched to her car, got in, then drove off in an angry cloud of dust. The knowledge that it would take Ramona a good twenty minutes to cross Cameron land and reach the highway made her briefly consider following in her car.

When Ramona's exit was nothing more than a wisp of dust in the distance, Tracy turned. Ty stood across the foyer from her, leaning against the wall, his arms crossed over his chest. His blue eyes were lit with satisfaction and a smile eased over his handsome mouth.

"It was one of the pleasures of my life to see you stand up to her and turn the tables. Not because I like to see anyone speak to their mother that way, and not because I don't realize that it must have hurt you to do it, but because of the simple pleasure of seeing someone as wronged as you were finally get a little justice." He paused and his voice lowered to a warm drawl. "You are an amazing woman, Tracy LeDeux, and I'm proud to know you."

Tracy exhaled a pent-up breath and gave him a smile that trembled. "Thank you for taking me away from Greg Parker that night and for being so tough and disapproving. For coming to the penthouse that next day, even after I'd wrecked your car and broke your door and refused to take your calls. I don't know how much longer I could have lived without that expensive disaster in the garage. Thank you for every single thing since that night. Especially for bringing me to this."

It was emotion that made her rush toward him and catch herself against him in a hard embrace. Relief made her almost giddy, and she laughed as he lifted her high and turned them both in a circle before he stopped and just hugged her to himself.

"It's all done now, Trace." He pressed a kiss in her hair then set her down and eased away enough to look down at her face. "I made reservations for dinner. Someplace where we can dress up and have a nice time. How does that sound to you?"

"Like I'd better get a shower and see what's in the closet," she bantered back.

"You go on ahead. I'll tell Maria and see you out here at about five."

The kiss he gave her then was long and deep, and somehow a preview of what he had in mind for the evening. Tracy stepped back when they moved away from each other and she stared at him, still amazed by the great good fortune that had brought her to Cameron Ranch.

His gruff, ''See you later,'' was a promise that warmed her.

It took Tracy days to fully get past the last confrontation with her mother. Not because it had traumatized her, but because it had been the act that forever put an end to her mother's power over her and blocked Ramona from ever being a presence in her life. The enormity of what she'd accomplished took some getting used to.

And as the days went by, she felt the peace and safety and magic of Cameron Ranch spread to the world at large. She felt safe and peaceful everywhere, and came to understand that it was a safety and peace she now carried inside her rather than a specific location on a map.

That feeling of peace and safety was ultimately put to the test one morning at breakfast when Ty announced that they were flying to Langtry Ranch.

''Kane's been calling off and on since you came here, wondering how you are, and he made me promise to bring you up to Langtry. Rio's pregnant and put out because he won't let her do ranch work, so she'd probably enjoy a break from the boredom of staying in the house with him all day. I know I'd be bored out of my mind cooped up with him.''

Tracy was immune to the joke he'd made about Kane being a bore for Rio to live with. She doubted very much that Rio would ever be bored with Kane, but she knew right away that Rio would hate spending all her time at the house. Rio lived for the outdoors, so she was probably stir-crazy.

But Ty had promised to take her to Langtry Ranch and she was suddenly sick with anxiety. The most terrible thing she'd ever done she'd done to Rio and Kane. She'd kept silent when she should have spoken. She could have spared them both the agony Ramona had instigated, but she hadn't until it was almost too late.

It didn't matter that both of them had forgiven her. She'd not been a helpless, dependent child. She'd been a twenty-one-year-old woman with a clear moral choice, and she'd let both of them down.

Ty's voice made her look over at him. "I haven't seen that look for a long time, baby, and I hate seeing it now. Kane and Rio bear you no ill will. They want to see you, they want to make sure you know everything's fine and they want to see for themselves that everything's fine with you."

Tracy put down her fork then and reached for the napkin on her lap to clutch it.

"I saw your letters on a backup file on the hard drive. It's a fine thing to do."

His statement made her glance away, faintly embarrassed that he'd found out. She'd written letters of apology to every department and jewelry store still in business and confessed the thefts she'd been a part of as a child. She'd deleted the file, then signed her name and enclosed checks for the amounts that she estimated would cover the things she could remember stealing. As a result, two of the department stores and one of the jewelers had promptly sent her credit cards and invitations to patronize their businesses.

She'd not had much luck tracking down the names of the people they'd visited when she was a child because she'd only been able to remember one last name. So far, she had no idea where that family had moved to, so there might not be a lot she could do to make up for those. She hadn't been part of her mother's blackmail schemes.

The thing with Rio and Kane was something else. She'd betrayed her stepbrother and wronged one of the few friends she'd ever had. There was no check she could write out that was large enough to pay for that and no letter of apology contrite enough.

She'd apologized and tried to fixed things, and because Kane and Rio were happily married now and expecting their first child, her efforts had succeeded. But she'd never felt that what she'd done had been enough, and her guilt over it had never gone away. She should have known she'd have to face it again sometime.

"We're together today, Tracy," Ty said softly,

"and we'll be together tomorrow. And the next day and the next, whether you let me take you to Langtry today or not. But you've come so far, Trace, you've done so much. Let's take care of this today, let's put this to rest, too."

Tracy couldn't speak, she couldn't look at him because her eyes were filling with tears and she didn't want to cry. But she couldn't keep from reaching across the table for his hand. He obliged and gave her fingers a reassuring squeeze.

Langtry Ranch didn't seem as massive as Cameron from the air, but once they were on the ground it seemed as large as a small country. One of the ranch hands met them at the airstrip and drove them to the main house.

Ty got out of the Jeep first, then turned to take Tracy's hand. He grabbed their overnight bags and they walked to the back patio. Guests came to the front door, but family always came to the back. Tracy didn't miss the subtle point Ty made by leading her to the back door instead of the front.

Kane and Rio both stepped out the door to meet them and her worries about going in the family door eased. Tracy was stiff at first and unable to speak. But Kane caught her up in a bear hug and swung her around until she was dizzy. By the second turn, she was hugging him back and her face was drenched with tears. Hugging Rio was more

precarious because her slim frame was now so
heavy with pregnancy that she had to lean forward
to hug the more petite Tracy.

Tracy's bemused, ''I can't believe it,'' was an
expression that covered both the sight of Rio's advanced pregnancy and the loving welcome they'd
given her.

''We can hardly believe it, either,'' Kane got in,
then pulled her against his side with a growl.
''Thought we'd never get you back here. That'd
better be the longest time you ever stay away.''

Tracy couldn't help that her arm went around
Kane's waist and the tears started a second time.

''Let's get you inside and find a hankie. Folks
lookin' on would think you were coming home to
a beating.''

Tracy did cry then, and Kane growled again and
ushered her into the house. Ty and Rio followed
and made conversation with each other while Kane
routed Tracy into the den. He grabbed a handful
of tissues from a box on his desk and pushed them
into her fingers. Tracy did her best to stop weeping
and mopped her face. When she finished, Kane
reached over and lifted her chin to lean close.

''Don't you ever again in your life run off and
not tell anyone where you're going,'' he said
sternly. ''For the rest of your days, I want to talk
to you at least once a month on the phone, and

you'd better let me see you in person at holidays and birthdays and anytime in between."

He smiled at the shock on her face, then released her chin and straightened. "So how's Cameron treating you down there at San Antone, little sister? I hear you learned to rope. Did you get a loop on him yet?"

Tracy stared, so overcome with emotion that she promptly burst into tears. Kane growled again, pulled her into his arms and put up with it as she cried into his shirtfront.

The night air had cooled in the hours Tracy and Rio had spent on the lounge chairs by the pool, talking. They'd talked everything out. Tracy had again made her apologies to both Kane and Rio, and this time when they assured her she was forgiven, she believed it. She was now completely at peace. She'd never experienced such a strong sense of family before and it soothed something in her that still craved to belong.

Eventually, Ty and Kane came out of the house and joined them. Kane had brought a bottle of champagne and a couple of glasses, Ty carried two more.

Rio sent Kane a contented smile. "Champagne. If this is a celebration, I'll have some."

"The doctor finally called me back and he gave permission for one glass," Kane said, then set the wineglasses aside on a low table to position the bottle and pop the cork. "Or you'd get bottled water."

"Says who? What are we celebrating?" Rio asked as she shifted awkwardly in the lounge chair to sit up straighter.

"Tracy's come home, we're about to birth a baby, and Cameron's got over the fact that I married you and he missed out," Kane told her, then glared meaningfully at Ty.

Rio sent Ty a surprised glance and said a soft, "Oh," before her gaze shifted to Tracy then swung back to her husband.

Kane's enigmatic, "I'll tell you about it later," to Rio's curious glance caught Tracy's attention, but before Tracy could follow the silent messages that suddenly flew between the other three, Kane popped the cork and a gush of champagne splattered the patio. In moments all their glasses were filled and Kane posed formally for the toast.

"This is for our family, however it got made," he began. "And the kindness of a good God who saw to it we all found each other and settled our differences. Also, this is for the love none of us can survive without, for the dear ones we've said goodbye to, and the dear ones who get to stay with us and give our lives meaning. And especially for the little ones who'll join us along the way. For the Langtry family, every one of them, which right now is the five of us, and the sacred ties that can't be broken.''

Kane stopped then, and grinned arrogantly, satisfied with his long speech. Ty's muttered, ''Running for office?'' and the giggles from Tracy and Rio made them all laugh and drink the toast.

Later, Tracy and Ty left Kane and Rio on the patio to go for a walk. The night was quiet and pleasant, and once they got away from the lights of the headquarters, the sky glittered overhead like scattered gems. Tracy still felt emotional about her reunion with Kane and Rio, so humbled and grateful that they were all at peace that she felt guilty for wanting more.

But she did want more. She wanted Ty Cameron. Seeing Kane and Rio's marriage up close, witnessing their happiness together and their joy over Rio's pregnancy had made Tracy envious for the same things. And Kane's mysterious words that night, that the Langtry family was the *five* of them, made her wonder whether Kane knew something or if he was just guessing. She knew he hadn't miscounted.

She'd loved Ty for months, and though she had more with him than she'd ever expected to have with any man, she wanted the rest now, she wanted to be his wife and everything that meant. But she couldn't get past the knowledge that there was an invisible boundary between them, some sort of line that Ty didn't cross.

She moved closer and snuggled her cheek against his arm as they walked hand in hand up the long ranch driveway. The craving to be as close to Ty as humanly possible was so compelling that it was all she could do to keep silent.

It seemed too greedy to want everything, but she couldn't forget how perfect Kane and Rio were together, how happy, how contented. She'd been hoping that Ty loved her and wanted a future with her, but today, seeing some of what was possible between a husband and wife, had only sharpened her desire.

Ty's voice was a warm drawl in the night air. "They look like diamonds up there, don't they?"

Tracy eased her cheek away from his arm and glanced up. Her eyes had adjusted to the darkness and she could make out Ty's face with surprising clarity. They'd stopped walking and now both of them stood looking up into the night sky.

"Some of them look so close out here you feel like you could just reach up and grab a handful," he said then and Tracy made an absent sound of agreement.

Ty lifted his arm and pointed. "See that one there? Just to the right of the Big Dipper? That bright one?"

Tracy had just located the one she thought he

meant when he seemed to pluck something out of the air above them. He brought his arm down and held his hand in front of her.

"See what I caught?" he said, and she heard the smile in his voice. She looked closer at what he held up between his thumb and finger. "Just for you, darlin' Tracy," he said in a low, gentle voice. "A little piece of Heaven to wear on your finger that says you belong to me for the rest of our lives."

It was a diamond ring! Tracy stared, stunned as he took her left hand. He lifted it between them and singled out her ring finger.

"So what do you say? I love you, Tracy LeDeux, and I want to live with you forever. I want us to be happy with each other, raise up our kids, then have them bring their babies home to us and their babies' babies." He paused a moment and his voice went lower. "I love you, and my life can only be happily-ever-after if you're always with me, if you'll be my wife."

Tracy was overwhelmed. She felt like laughing and crying at once. "I've loved you so long," she said shakily, dazed by what he'd said. "I want to be with you forever, too, I want everything with you. Everything."

Ty slid the ring on her finger and grabbed her up in a hug that lifted her off her feet. Wildly, he kissed her, and she matched him kiss for kiss. Ty's hat landed on the ground behind him and the stars overhead seemed to whirl in a joyous dance.

Ty finally staggered with the need for air and they broke off the kiss to hold each other tightly.

"Lord a mercy, Miz Tracy, you sure know how to make a man go weak in the knees."

Tracy laughed happily in his arms, her heart so full that she couldn't help the warm tears that streaked down her face.

"I'll give you four weeks to put together enough of a wedding to make you happy," he growled with mock sternness. "Kane says he'll give you away here at Langtry if we want, and he knows the name of a good wedding planner to make the rush easier to live through."

Tracy drew back and studied his face in the starlight. "Do Kane and Rio know you were going to propose?"

She could see his smile. "Rio said she'd stay awake long enough to find out what your answer was. Kane and I already worked out names for our kids, because it turns out we like the same ones and don't want duplicates."

Tracy laughed at that and hugged him tightly, so overwhelmed with love and joy that her heart saw the bright promise of the future as clearly as a beautiful photograph.

NEARLYWEDS

Almost at the altar— will these *nearly*weds become *newly*weds?

Harlequin Romance® is delighted to invite you to some special weddings! Yet these are no ordinary weddings. Our beautiful brides and gorgeous grooms only *nearly* make it to the altar—before fate intervenes.

But the story doesn't end there....
Find out what happens in these tantalizingly emotional novels!

Authors to look out for include:

**Leigh Michaels—The Bridal Swap
Liz Fielding—His Runaway Bride
Janelle Denison—The Wedding Secret
Renee Roszel—Finally a Groom
Caroline Anderson—The Impetuous Bride**

Available wherever Harlequin books are sold.

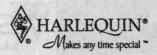

HARLEQUIN®
Makes any time special ™